THE FRAGMENTS WITHIN

THE FRAGMENTS WITHIN

DAVID OLUBIYI

Dabim Support Services Inc

Contents

For those who have journeyed through the depths of struggle, for those who have embraced vulnerability in the pursuit of healing, and for those who continue to discover the fragments of their true selves. May your path be illuminated by the light of resilience and the beauty of self-discovery. This book is dedicated to you.

I

❧

Broken Pieces

Emily gazed at herself in the mirror, her mask of smiles firmly in place. To the outside world, she appeared radiant, a picture of contentment and joy. Yet, beneath that carefully crafted façade, a tempest raged within her. It was a storm of emotions, fueled by the relentless grip of addiction.

Her eyes, usually sparkling with warmth, now held a hint of weariness. The weight of her secret burden tugged at her spirit, threatening to shatter the fragile equilibrium she maintained. Each smile she mustered became an artful disguise, concealing the chaos that consumed her soul.

The mask she wore was not born out of deceit, but rather out of a desperate desire to protect those she loved. Emily feared that if her true struggles were exposed, they would be burdened with her pain. So, she carried the weight of her addiction in silence, alone in her suffering.

Days turned into weeks, weeks into months, and the cycle

of addiction persisted. The allure of her vice gnawed at her willpower, demanding surrender to its seductive embrace. It whispered promises of temporary solace, an escape from the overwhelming weight of her existence.

In the solitude of her room, Emily would often find herself succumbing to the lure. The allure of the substance would beckon her with an intoxicating melody, drowning out the whispers of reason and self-restraint. It became a refuge from the demands of the outside world, a fleeting sanctuary where she could briefly numb the pain that plagued her.

But with each passing moment of surrender, Emily felt herself slipping further away from the person she longed to be. She yearned for connection, for authenticity, yet addiction wove a web of deception that distanced her from her true self. It shackled her with invisible chains, binding her to a never-ending cycle of craving and remorse.

She longed to break free, to reclaim her life from the clutches of addiction. Yet, she was ensnared in a paradoxical dance, simultaneously craving liberation and fearing the void it might leave behind. The familiarity of her addiction provided a twisted sense of comfort, a deceptive solace that masked the underlying pain.

Emily's addiction had become a specter that haunted her, casting its shadow over every aspect of her life. It infiltrated her relationships, tarnishing moments of joy and staining the tapestry of her existence. She yearned for release from its grasp, for a chance to mend the broken pieces of her soul.

As she stood before the mirror, Emily recognized the toll her addiction had taken on her spirit. The exhaustion etched upon her face was a reflection of the battles fought in the shadows. She longed for the day when her smile would no longer require a mask, when her laughter would ring true, unburdened by the weight of her secret struggle.

In the depths of her despair, a flicker of hope emerged. It whispered softly, a gentle reminder that healing was possible, that the shattered fragments of her soul could be reassembled. With each passing day, Emily grew more determined to embark on the journey towards redemption, towards unmasking her true self.

Though the road ahead appeared daunting, Emily clung to the belief that within the broken pieces lay the potential for wholeness. She yearned for the day when her smile would reflect genuine joy, when her laughter would ring true. The mask she wore would no longer be necessary, for the storms within would be stilled, and the shattered fragments of her soul would be lovingly reassembled.

With a deep breath and a newfound resolve, Emily stepped forward, ready to confront the darkness that had held her captive for far too long. The journey towards healing and self-discovery awaited her, beckoning her to embrace the shattered pieces and forge a path towards restoration. It was time to peel back the layers, to reveal the rawness beneath the mask, and to embrace the transformative power of healing.

And so, with determination in her heart and a glimmer of hope in her eyes, Emily set forth on her journey. It would be a journey of courage and resilience, of facing the demons within and learning to mend the broken pieces. The path would be arduous, but she knew that within the depths of her struggle, lay the seeds of her redemption.

Emily sat alone in her dimly lit room, her gaze fixed on

the flickering candle flame before her. The burden of her addiction weighed heavily upon her shoulders, pressing down with an unrelenting force. It was a weight she carried in solitude, hidden from the prying eyes of those she held dear. The thought of revealing her struggles to them filled her with a deep sense of dread and fear.

In the depths of her being, Emily longed for connection and understanding. She yearned for someone to listen without judgment, to hold her hand through the darkest of nights. But the shame and stigma that surrounded addiction gripped her heart with icy fingers, silencing her cries for help.

She had witnessed the repercussions of vulnerability in the past - the disapproving glances, the hushed whispers, the disappointment etched upon the faces of her loved ones. It was a pain she couldn't bear to inflict upon them again. And so, she donned the mask of strength, concealing her inner turmoil behind a carefully constructed façade.

The weight of her secret burden was suffocating, like an invisible chain that bound her to her addiction. The walls of isolation grew higher with each passing day, further entrenching her in the cycle of shame and silence. She believed that she had to face her demons alone, that her struggles were hers to bear in solitude.

But in the depths of her despair, a glimmer of hope flickered. It was a whisper, urging her to consider the possibility of sharing her truth, of reaching out to those who cared for her. The voice reminded her that true healing could only begin when she allowed herself to be seen, flaws and all.

The fear of rejection and judgment still loomed large, but Emily realized that the burden of her secret was far heavier than the potential consequences of opening up. She yearned for authentic connection, for the freedom that came with vulnerability. It was time to shed the weight of her addiction and find solace in the embrace of compassion and understanding.

With trembling hands, Emily mustered the courage to reach out to a trusted friend. As she poured her heart out, the words spilled forth like a torrential downpour, washing away the walls she had meticulously built. The weight on her shoulders began to ease, as if the mere act of sharing had already lightened the load.

To her surprise, her friend listened with empathy and love, embracing her without judgment. The air between them became a sanctuary, where her struggles were met with understanding and support. In that moment, Emily realized that the burden of secrets was not meant to be carried alone.

Emboldened by this newfound connection, Emily gradually shared her journey with others who mattered to her. Each confession became a step towards liberation, a testament to her strength and resilience. With each person she trusted, the weight of her addiction grew lighter, and she discovered that she was not alone in her struggles.

Through sharing her truth, Emily unearthed a network of love and support that had been waiting patiently for her to embrace it. The veil of shame began to dissolve, replaced by a newfound sense of acceptance and belonging. It was within the embrace of her loved ones that she found the courage to face her addiction head-on, to seek the help she so desperately needed.

Emily realized that carrying the burden of her addiction

alone was an unnecessary weight, one that only served to prolong her suffering. Opening up allowed her to tap into the strength of her support system, to gather the courage necessary for her healing journey. In vulnerability, she found resilience, and in shared struggles, she discovered the power of human connection.

As Emily continued her journey towards healing and self-discovery, she carried with her the invaluable lesson that burdens are lighter when shared, and that true strength lies in the ability to ask for help. No longer burdened by the weight of her secrets, she embarked on a path illuminated by compassion, understanding, and the unwavering support of those who loved her.

The allure of her addiction grew stronger with each passing day, its seductive whispers enveloping Emily's thoughts and tugging at her weakened resolve. The grip it held on her seemed to tighten, like invisible shackles constricting her freedom. The temptation was an ever-present companion, lurking in the shadows, waiting for a moment of vulnerability to pounce.

Emily had tasted moments of freedom from her addiction, glimpses of a life untouched by its destructive power. But as the days turned into weeks, she found herself ensnared once again, trapped in a cycle of cravings and remorse. The comfort and solace it promised seemed irresistible, a temporary respite from the pain and chaos that plagued her.

In moments of weakness, the allure of her addiction would whisper sweet promises, its persuasive voice echoing in the depths of her mind. It painted vivid pictures of blissful escape, numbing the pain that threatened to overwhelm her.

The weight of her emotions felt unbearable, and her addiction appeared as the only refuge, a false sanctuary she could turn to for relief.

Her resistance crumbled like sand between her fingers, as the urge to succumb to the pull of her addiction grew stronger. Rationality and reason lost their footing, drowned out by the siren song that beckoned her towards a temporary bliss. Each time she managed to break free, it seemed as if the addiction clawed its way back with renewed vigor, its hold tightening with each relapse.

Emily found herself in a battle, a war waged within her own mind and body. The rational part of her yearned for freedom, for liberation from the chains that bound her. She knew deep down that her addiction only perpetuated the cycle of pain and despair. But the allure of temporary escape, the numbing of her emotions, proved difficult to resist.

In moments of clarity, she would remind herself of the consequences, the wreckage left in the wake of her addiction. She saw the toll it took on her relationships, the trust that was eroded, and the disappointment etched upon the faces of her loved ones. Yet, even armed with this knowledge, the temptation's grip remained steadfast, refusing to release its hold.

As she struggled to resist, Emily sought solace in the support of those who understood her journey. She leaned on her support network, reaching out to friends, counselors, and fellow travelers on the path to recovery. They became beacons of strength, guiding her through the darkest moments, reminding her of the light that awaited on the other side of her addiction.

But despite the encouragement and understanding, there were moments when Emily felt utterly alone. The weight of her cravings and the intense desire for escape pressed down upon her, threatening to engulf her entirely. She found herself standing at the precipice, torn between the longing for freedom and the magnetic pull of her addiction.

In these moments of vulnerability, she had to dig deep within herself, tapping into the wellspring of strength that resided within her. She reminded herself of her journey thus far, of the progress she had made and the battles she had already won. She clung to the hope that resided within her, the belief that healing was possible, that she was capable of breaking free from the chains that held her captive.

With each passing day, Emily fought the temptation's grip with renewed determination. She sought healthier coping mechanisms, turning to therapy, meditation, and creative outlets to channel her emotions. She surrounded herself with positive influences and embraced a lifestyle that nurtured her well-being.

It was a long and arduous journey, marked by setbacks and triumphs, but Emily refused to surrender to the allure of her addiction. She knew that true freedom lay not in its false promises, but in the courageous act of resisting its temptations.

As time went on, the grip of her addiction began to loosen. The cravings, though still present, became more manageable. Emily discovered a newfound strength within herself, an inner resilience that grew with each victory over temptation.

Through sheer determination, unwavering support, and a deep desire for transformation, Emily inched closer to reclaiming her life. She learned that resisting the temptation's grip required immense courage, self-compassion, and an unwavering commitment to her own well-being.

And as she stood on the precipice of a new day, Emily could feel the allure of her addiction slowly losing its power. In its place, a glimmer of hope emerged, illuminating her path towards healing and self-discovery. She was no longer defined by her addiction but by her strength to resist it.

With each passing day, Emily grew stronger, embracing the challenges that came her way. The allure of her addiction would forever be a part of her story, a reminder of the battles she fought and the resilience she cultivated. And as she continued on her journey, she carried with her the knowledge that true freedom was not found in escape but in the unwavering commitment to her own well-being.

Emily stood at the precipice of her choices, the consequences of her addiction unfurling before her like a haunting tapestry. The once enticing allure now revealed its true nature, leaving a trail of destruction in its wake. The life she had known was crumbling, and she was forced to confront the consequences of her actions.

As the haze of addiction lifted, Emily began to see the toll it had taken on her life. Relationships that were once vibrant and full of love had withered under the weight of her addiction. Trust had been eroded, leaving behind scars that seemed impossible to heal. She was faced with the wreckage of broken promises and shattered dreams, a stark reminder of the path she had chosen.

The consequences extended far beyond her personal relationships. Her physical and mental health bore the marks of her addiction. Sleepless nights and neglected self-care had left her drained, both physically and emotionally. The toll on her body was undeniable, and she could no longer ignore the signs of neglect.

As she surveyed the wreckage, a deep sense of regret washed over Emily. She questioned the choices that had led her down this destructive path. The allure that had once promised solace and escape now revealed itself as a false beacon, leading her astray. She wondered how she had allowed herself to be consumed by something so damaging, something that had taken so much from her.

Guilt and shame became constant companions, their whispers echoing in her mind. She grappled with the weight of responsibility, knowing that her actions had not only harmed herself but also those who cared for her. The realization was a bitter pill to swallow, a painful awakening to the consequences of her addiction.

In the depths of her despair, Emily found herself at a crossroads. She could either continue down the path of self-destruction, allowing the consequences to swallow her whole, or she could choose to rise from the ashes and rebuild her life. It was a daunting decision, but she knew deep down that she deserved better than the wreckage before her.

With the support of her loved ones and the lessons learned from her mistakes, Emily began to take the first steps towards redemption. She sought help, reaching out to professionals who could guide her on the path to recovery. Therapy became a lifeline, offering her the tools to navigate the complex web of emotions that had led her astray.

It was a humbling journey of self-reflection and introspection. Emily confronted the underlying pain and trauma that had fueled her addiction, facing the demons she had long tried to escape. She learned to sit with discomfort, to face the consequences of her actions head-on, and to take responsibility for her own healing.

The road to rebuilding was not without obstacles. There were moments of doubt, moments when the weight of her past threatened to pull her back into old patterns. But she clung to the hope that had ignited within her, the belief that she could forge a new path, one rooted in self-love and resilience.

As the consequences of her addiction continued to unveil themselves, Emily found a newfound sense of clarity. She saw the importance of making amends, not only to those she had hurt but also to herself. She embarked on a journey of self-forgiveness, recognizing that healing required compassion and a willingness to let go of the past.

With each step forward, Emily reclaimed pieces of herself that had been lost to addiction. She discovered strength in vulnerability, courage in facing her mistakes, and a deep reservoir of resilience that allowed her to rise from the ashes of self-destruction. The consequences of her choices became catalysts for growth, pushing her towards a life of authenticity and purpose.

Emily's journey of self-discovery was not without scars, but they served as reminders of the battles she had fought and the lessons she had learned. The consequences of her addiction had unveiled a path to redemption, a chance to rebuild her life on a foundation of self-awareness and self-love. And as she continued to navigate the twists and turns of her healing journey, Emily carried with her the knowledge that she had the power to shape her own destiny, one choice at a time.

In the midst of the darkness that enveloped Emily's life, a tiny flicker of hope began to emerge, like a distant star piercing through the night sky. It was a fragile glimmer, barely noticeable at first, but it held within it the potential for a better future. Amidst the wreckage of her addiction, Emily started to recognize the need for change, and with it, a growing determination to seek out the first rays of hope.

As she stood at the crossroads of her life, Emily felt a stirring deep within her soul. The consequences of her choices had left her wounded and weary, but within the depths of her despair, a yearning for something different began to take hold. It was a whisper, a gentle nudge urging her to rise above the darkness and embrace the possibility of a brighter tomorrow.

The glimmer of hope took many forms. It manifested in the moments of clarity when she glimpsed the person she could become, untethered from the chains of addiction. It shone through the kind words of a friend who believed in her, reminding her that she was worthy of love and forgiveness. It resonated in the stories of others who had overcome their own struggles, offering a glimpse of the transformative power of healing.

As Emily started to explore the possibility of change, she encountered the first signs of hope in unexpected places. She stumbled upon support groups where she met individuals who had faced similar battles and emerged victorious. Their stories became beacons of inspiration, testaments to the resilience of the human spirit.

Through therapy and self-reflection, Emily began to uncover the underlying wounds that had led her down the path of addiction. She realized that her addiction had been a desperate attempt to numb the pain and fill the void within her. With this newfound understanding, she embarked on a journey of self-discovery and healing, determined to rewrite her story.

The glimmers of hope grew stronger as Emily started to make positive changes in her life. She surrounded herself with a community of individuals who uplifted and supported her, creating a network of love and encouragement. She discovered healthy coping mechanisms to replace her destructive habits, engaging in activities that nurtured her mind, body, and soul.

Each small step forward brought her closer to the life she longed for—a life filled with purpose, fulfillment, and genuine connections. The glimmer of hope illuminated her path, guiding her through the challenging moments and reminding her of the infinite possibilities that lay ahead.

With time, Emily witnessed the impact of her efforts. The dark clouds of addiction gradually gave way to rays of light, casting warmth upon her soul. She felt the weight of shame and regret slowly dissipate, replaced by a growing sense of self-compassion and forgiveness.

As she continued to walk the path of recovery, Emily discovered an inner strength she had never known existed. She recognized that change was not a linear journey but a series of small victories and setbacks. In moments of doubt, she drew upon the glimmer of hope, holding onto it as a reminder of her own resilience and the potential for transformation.

The glimmer of hope became her guiding light, leading her through the darkness and propelling her towards a future filled with promise. It whispered to her heart, urging her to keep going, to keep striving for the life she deserved. It reminded her that change was possible, that she had the power to shape her own destiny.

As Emily embraced the glimmers of hope that illuminated her path, she discovered that hope was not just an abstract concept but a tangible force that could ignite her spirit. It propelled her forward, giving her the strength to face the challenges that lay ahead and to continue on her journey of healing and self-discovery.

With every step she took, the glimmer of hope grew brighter, enveloping her in its gentle glow. It became the driving force behind her transformation, reminding her that even in the darkest of times, there was always a ray of light waiting to be found. And with unwavering determination, Emily set forth, chasing the glimmer of hope and embracing the possibility of a better, brighter future.

2

The Tempest Unveiled

Emily found herself in the midst of a tempest, a swirling storm of emotions that threatened to consume her. The very feelings she had long tried to escape through her addiction now demanded her attention, urging her to confront them head-on. It was a daunting task, but she knew deep down that it was a necessary step on her path to healing.

As the storm raged within, Emily braved the turbulent sea of her emotions. She allowed herself to feel the full force of her pain, her anger, her fear, and her sadness. It was an uncomfortable journey, for these emotions had been suppressed for far too long, buried beneath layers of addiction and denial. But she understood that in order to heal, she needed to face them, to give them a voice.

Conversations that had long been avoided now became vital lifelines. Emily sought out the needed discussions, opening up to trusted friends, family members, and professionals.

She shared the depths of her struggles, the wounds that had been festering beneath the surface. These conversations became bridges, connecting her to others who could offer empathy, understanding, and guidance.

In the safety of these discussions, Emily peeled back the layers of her pain, exposing the raw vulnerability that lay within. She explored the roots of her addiction, delving into past traumas, unresolved conflicts, and unmet needs. It was a process of self-discovery, uncovering the layers of her identity and understanding the emotional voids she had sought to fill.

The conversations she engaged in were not always easy. They required her to confront uncomfortable truths, to acknowledge her role in her own struggles. She had to face the consequences of her actions, both for herself and for those who cared about her. It was a humbling experience, but one that was necessary for her growth and transformation.

Through these conversations, Emily began to understand that her addiction had served as a coping mechanism—a way to numb the pain, to escape the overwhelming emotions that threatened to drown her. She recognized that her addiction had been a misguided attempt to find solace and control in a chaotic world.

As she navigated these discussions, Emily discovered the power of vulnerability. She realized that by sharing her story and allowing herself to be seen in her rawest form, she could find connection and support. It was through these conversations that she started to build a network of understanding and compassion, a support system that could help her weather the storm.

The tempestuous emotions that once fueled her addiction

now became catalysts for self-discovery and growth. She learned to sit with her discomfort, to embrace the depths of her emotions without judgment or the need for escape. She recognized that these emotions were not her enemies but messengers, guiding her towards the areas of her life that needed attention and healing.

As the storm raged within, Emily discovered her own resilience. She realized that she had the strength to face her emotions, to ride the waves of uncertainty, and to emerge stronger on the other side. These conversations became lifelines, anchoring her to the present moment and reminding her of the power she held within herself.

With each needed conversation, Emily's understanding of herself deepened. She began to recognize the patterns and triggers that had perpetuated her addiction, and she developed healthier ways to navigate her emotions. She learned the importance of self-care, of setting boundaries, and of seeking support when needed.

The storm raged on, but Emily no longer feared its power. She had confronted the tempestuous emotions within her, understanding that they were a natural part of being human. They no longer held the same control over her, for she had learned to harness their energy and transform it into personal growth and healing.

As the storm slowly subsided, Emily emerged from the tempest stronger and wiser. She had weathered the turmoil of her emotions and engaged in the needed conversations that had paved the way for self-discovery. The path ahead was still uncertain, but she now possessed the tools and resilience to face whatever challenges lay in wait.

The storm within had been unveiled, and in its wake, Emily found a newfound sense of empowerment and clarity. She understood that by embracing her emotions and engaging in the necessary conversations, she was taking an active role in her own healing and transformation. And with renewed strength, she pressed forward, ready to confront whatever tempests may come her way.

Emily sat before her blank notebook, her pen poised above the paper. It was time to release the weight of her past, to unburden herself through the power of confession. She had decided to write her memoir, a raw and honest account of her journey through addiction, healing, and self-discovery. In the act of putting pen to paper, she hoped to find clarity and a sense of liberation.

With each word she penned, Emily opened the floodgates of her soul. She delved into the depths of her experiences, exploring the darkest corners of her addiction and the moments of triumph that had brought her to where she stood now. The act of confessing her truths on paper allowed her to confront the shame and guilt that had lingered within her for far too long.

The memoir became her sanctuary, a safe space where she could pour out her heart without judgment or fear of rejection. She bared her soul, revealing the struggles, the triumphs, and the countless moments of vulnerability that had shaped her journey. Through her words, she sought to shine a light on the realities of addiction, to offer hope to those who may find solace in her story.

As Emily chronicled her experiences, she gained a newfound perspective on her own life. The act of writing allowed her to step back and witness the narrative unfold from a different vantage point. It provided a sense of distance and objectivity, enabling her to see the patterns, the triggers, and the choices that had led her down the treacherous path of addiction.

In the process of confession, Emily discovered that her story held transformative power not only for herself but also for others. As she poured her heart onto the pages, she realized that her words had the potential to inspire, to offer comfort to those who were facing similar struggles. The vulnerability and authenticity of her story became a beacon of hope, reminding others that they were not alone.

Through the act of confessing her truth, Emily found clarity and understanding. As she revisited her past, she could see the trajectory of her journey and the lessons learned along the way. Writing her memoir became a form of self-reflection, an opportunity to make sense of the tangled threads of her experiences and to find meaning in the chaos.

The process of confession was not without its challenges. Emily grappled with the fear of judgment and the vulnerability of exposing her innermost struggles to the world. But she pressed forward, knowing that her story held the potential to touch lives and ignite conversations that were often kept in the shadows.

As she neared the conclusion of her memoir, Emily felt a sense of release and liberation. The act of confession had allowed her to shed the weight of her past, to let go of the secrets that had held her captive. She realized that by sharing her story, she had taken back control of her narrative and reclaimed her voice.

In the pages of her memoir, Emily found redemption. She discovered that her experiences, both the triumphs and the failures, were integral to her growth and self-discovery. Through the power of her words, she had transformed her pain into purpose, her journey into a beacon of hope.

And as she closed her notebook, Emily felt a sense of completion. The act of confession had granted her the clarity she had sought. She knew that her story was not just a memoir but a testament to the resilience of the human spirit, a reminder that healing and self-discovery were possible for anyone who dared to embark on the journey.

With her memoir complete, Emily was ready to share her story with the world. She hoped that her words would reach those who needed them most, that her vulnerability would serve as a catalyst for healing and self-reflection. The power of confession had set her free, and she was determined to help others find their own liberation through the power of their truth.

Emily stood at the precipice of her healing journey, her heart heavy with the weight of past mistakes. It was time to face the shadows of her actions, to acknowledge the pain she had caused and seek redemption. With humility and a sincere desire for change, she embarked on a path of self-forgiveness and the pursuit of redemption.

In the solitude of reflection, Emily confronted the consequences of her addiction and the impact it had on herself and those around her. She recognized the pain she had inflicted upon loved ones, the broken trust, and the shattered relationships. With a heavy heart, she accepted the reality of her past actions, no longer willing to ignore or diminish their significance.

The first step towards redemption was acknowledging her mistakes. Emily took ownership of her actions, recognizing that she had been driven by her addiction and the misguided choices it led her to make. She allowed herself to feel the weight of remorse, to face the discomfort that arose from confronting her past head-on.

Seeking forgiveness required vulnerability and a willingness to make amends. Emily reached out to those she had hurt, expressing her remorse and acknowledging the pain she had caused. She understood that forgiveness was not guaranteed, that healing the wounds she had inflicted would take time and patience. But she was committed to the process, ready to do whatever it took to mend the broken bonds.

In her quest for redemption, Emily turned inward, exploring the depths of her own self-forgiveness. She recognized that in order to move forward, she needed to release the burdens of guilt and shame that weighed upon her. Through therapy, self-reflection, and acts of self-compassion, she started to unravel the layers of self-blame and judgment.

The path to self-forgiveness was not linear. There were moments of doubt and resistance, times when the pain of her past threatened to overwhelm her. But Emily persevered, drawing strength from the knowledge that she was on a journey of growth and transformation. She surrounded herself with supportive individuals who encouraged her in her pursuit of redemption.

As she sought forgiveness from others and herself, Emily embraced the process of atonement. She engaged in acts of kindness and service, seeking to make a positive impact in the lives of those around her. She committed herself to personal growth and self-improvement, knowing that the best way to make amends was to become a better version of herself.

Redemption was not about erasing the past or pretending it never happened. It was about acknowledging the pain and mistakes, taking responsibility, and actively working towards change. Emily understood that seeking redemption was an ongoing journey, a continuous process of growth and self-reflection.

Through her actions and commitment to change, Emily began to experience glimpses of redemption. She witnessed the healing that could arise from genuine remorse and sincere efforts to make amends. Relationships started to mend, trust slowly rebuilt, and she started to see glimmers of forgiveness from those she had hurt.

But perhaps the most profound redemption came from within. As Emily embraced self-forgiveness, she discovered a newfound sense of freedom and self-acceptance. She realized that her past mistakes did not define her, but rather served as catalysts for growth and transformation. She recognized that redemption was not about erasing the past, but about learning from it and using it as a stepping stone towards a brighter future.

With each step she took on her journey towards redemption, Emily felt a renewed sense of purpose and hope. She knew that she could not change the past, but she could shape her future through her actions and choices. Seeking forgiveness and embracing self-forgiveness became beacons of light, guiding her towards a life of healing, growth, and ultimately, redemption.

Emily embarked on a profound journey of self-discovery as she delved deep into the underlying triggers and influences that had perpetuated her addiction. She understood that in order to heal, she needed to unmask these hidden forces and gain a deeper understanding of their power over her.

With a determined spirit, Emily began to unravel the intricate web of triggers that had fueled her addiction. She recognized that triggers were not limited to specific external factors, but also encompassed internal emotions, past traumas, and patterns of behavior. Through therapy, introspection, and self-reflection, she sought to uncover the root causes that had kept her trapped in the cycle of addiction.

Emily explored the connection between her addiction and her emotions. She discovered that certain feelings, such as stress, anxiety, loneliness, or even moments of joy, had triggered her cravings for substances or unhealthy behaviors. By becoming aware of these emotional triggers, she gained the power to address them head-on and develop healthier coping mechanisms.

She also examined the role of past traumas and unresolved wounds in perpetuating her addiction. Emily recognized that her addiction had served as a means of escape from the pain and memories that haunted her. Through therapy, she courageously confronted these traumas, allowing herself to process the emotions associated with them and work towards healing and resolution.

In addition to internal triggers, Emily explored the external influences that had played a part in her addiction. She examined the social environments, relationships, and societal pressures that had contributed to her destructive behaviors. By understanding these external triggers, she became better equipped to navigate challenging situations and make conscious choices aligned with her healing journey.

As Emily unmasked the triggers, she realized that awareness alone was not enough. She needed to develop alternative strategies and healthy coping mechanisms to replace the destructive patterns she had relied upon in the past. Through therapy, support groups, and self-help resources, she learned new ways to manage her emotions, deal with stress, and find solace in healthy outlets.

Self-reflection became a vital tool in Emily's journey of unmasking triggers. She took time to examine her own thought processes, beliefs, and self-perceptions. By challenging negative self-talk and cultivating self-compassion, she empowered herself to break free from the destructive cycles that had kept her trapped.

The process of unmasking triggers was not without its challenges. Emily encountered moments of resistance, moments where the discomfort of facing her vulnerabilities threatened to pull her back into familiar patterns. But she persisted, fueled by her desire for healing and a life free from the grips of addiction.

As Emily gained clarity on the triggers that had influenced her addiction, she began to reclaim her power. Armed with this knowledge, she could recognize the warning signs and proactively engage in self-care and healthy coping strategies. She built a support network of understanding and compassionate individuals who could provide guidance and encouragement along her journey.

Unmasking the triggers became a transformative experience for Emily. It allowed her to break free from the chains of her addiction and take control of her own narrative. With newfound awareness and resilience, she faced each trigger with strength and determination, refusing to let them dictate her path any longer.

As Emily continued to unmask the triggers, she understood that healing was not a linear process. It required patience, self-compassion, and a commitment to growth. But armed with her newfound knowledge and a deep understanding of herself, she was ready to face the challenges that lay ahead and pave the way for a future filled with healing, empowerment, and self-discovery.

In the depths of her healing journey, Emily discovered an unexpected source of solace and transformation—the power of writing. As she put pen to paper, she embarked on a journey of self-expression and storytelling that would become a form of therapy, offering her a profound sense of healing and self-discovery.

Writing became Emily's sanctuary, a space where she could pour her thoughts, emotions, and experiences onto the page without judgment or limitations. Through the act of writing, she found a channel to release the turmoil within her soul, allowing her to make sense of her journey and find meaning in her pain.

As the words flowed from her pen, Emily experienced a catharsis unlike any other. Writing became a form of release, a way to untangle the intricate threads of her thoughts and emotions. Through storytelling, she could explore the depths of her addiction, the complexities of her healing process, and the moments of self-discovery that shaped her transformation.

The act of writing allowed Emily to delve into the raw and vulnerable aspects of her experiences, confronting the truth with unflinching honesty. She explored the nuances of her emotions, the moments of despair, and the flickers of hope that danced within her. Through storytelling, she was able to give voice to her pain and triumphs, weaving a narrative that was uniquely hers.

In the process of writing, Emily discovered that her words held the power to heal not only herself but also others who resonated with her story. She recognized the universality of human struggles and the healing potential of shared experiences. Through her storytelling, she sought to inspire, uplift, and offer a ray of hope to those who may be walking a similar path.

Writing became a form of self-reflection for Emily, allowing her to gain insights into her own growth and transformation. As she revisited her past through the written word, she could witness the progress she had made, the lessons she had learned, and the person she was becoming. The act of writing provided a mirror through which she could see her own resilience and the strength that had emerged from the depths of her struggles.

Through the process of writing, Emily found a sense of empowerment. She realized that her voice mattered, that her story held value and had the potential to impact others. She embraced her role as a storyteller, understanding that her words could bring comfort, provoke thought, and ignite conversations that were often kept in the shadows.

Writing became a constant companion in Emily's healing journey. Whether through journaling, poetry, or the creation of her memoir, she allowed the written word to guide her through the ups and downs of her path. The act of writing became an anchor, providing her with a sense of purpose, clarity, and self-expression.

As Emily witnessed the therapeutic power of writing, she encouraged others on their healing journeys to explore their own forms of self-expression. She recognized that writing was just one avenue of creative expression, and each person had their unique way of finding solace and healing through art, music, dance, or any other creative outlet.

Through the process of writing, Emily discovered the transformative power of self-expression and storytelling. It became her therapy, her refuge, and her guide towards healing and self-discovery. As she continued to write her story, she realized that her words had the power to shape her narrative, rewrite her past, and inspire a future filled with growth, resilience, and the unwavering belief in the transformative power of the human spirit.

3

The Journey Begins

Emily recognized the importance of seeking wisdom and guidance from those who had walked a similar path. Turning to literature, she immersed herself in the works of philosophers, poets, and writers who had grappled with addiction and the quest for self-discovery.

In the depths of her addiction, Emily had felt isolated, as if she were the only one wrestling with the demons that plagued her. But through literature, she discovered a vast community of souls who had experienced similar struggles and had found solace, understanding, and enlightenment within the pages of their written words.

She delved into the works of philosophers, such as Nietzsche, who explored the depths of human suffering and the transformative power of overcoming adversity. Their philosophical musings served as a guiding light, offering insights into the nature of addiction, the complexities of human existence, and the search for meaning in the face of adversity.

Emily found solace in the verses of poets who had bared their souls and grappled with their own addictions. She turned to the works of Sylvia Plath, who artfully captured the anguish and despair that can consume one's being, and yet also glimpsed moments of transcendent beauty and hope. Through the words of these poets, Emily discovered the healing power of poetry as a medium for self-expression and catharsis.

Literature became Emily's companion, a trusted confidant who offered solace and understanding. She devoured memoirs and autobiographies of individuals who had battled addiction, finding inspiration in their journeys of recovery and self-discovery. Their stories served as reminders that healing was possible, that redemption could be found, and that one's past did not define their future.

Through literature, Emily gained a deeper understanding of her own struggles and the underlying patterns that had perpetuated her addiction. The words of these authors resonated within her, giving voice to emotions she had long suppressed and shedding light on the complexities of human nature.

As she immersed herself in the writings of those who had traversed the treacherous terrain of addiction and self-discovery, Emily began to weave the threads of her own narrative. She found solace in their words, recognizing that she was not alone in her journey. The shared experiences of these authors validated her own struggles and offered a roadmap towards healing and self-transformation.

Reading became more than a mere pastime for Emily—

it became a transformative experience. Each page turned was an opportunity for introspection, a chance to reflect on her own journey and contemplate the lessons embedded within the text. The wisdom she gleaned from literature provided her with new perspectives, alternative ways of thinking, and a renewed sense of hope.

In her pursuit of wisdom, Emily also sought out contemporary writers who had explored addiction and self-discovery in their works. She delved into novels, essays, and articles that tackled the complexities of addiction, the human psyche, and the search for personal growth. These modern voices expanded her understanding and provided fresh insights into her own struggles.

As Emily absorbed the words of these literary masters, she began to piece together the puzzle of her own healing journey. Their wisdom seeped into her soul, igniting a fire within her to confront her addiction, delve into her past, and seek the profound truths that would guide her towards healing and self-discovery.

With each book she read, Emily felt herself growing stronger, more resilient. The words of these writers became her companions, her mentors, and her guides. Their stories echoed within her, propelling her forward on her quest for self-transformation.

Through literature, Emily discovered that wisdom could be found in the written word. The insights of philosophers, the poetry of souls bared, and the stories of those who had overcome addiction became beacons of light, illuminating her path towards healing and self-discovery.

As Emily turned the pages of her literary journey, she knew

that the wisdom she gained would not only shape her own life but also become a beacon of hope for others who grappled with addiction and sought their own path to healing. She understood that literature held the power to connect hearts, inspire change, and spark a revolution of self-discovery.

In the vast world of literature, Emily found her refuge, her sanctuary, and her catalyst for growth. And with each book she devoured, she moved closer to uncovering the truths that would set her free.

As Emily continued her journey of healing and self-discovery, she turned to the timeless wisdom contained within classic literature. Immersed in the pages of novels and plays, she found solace and guidance, drawing parallels between her own experiences and the struggles of literary characters who had faced their own trials and tribulations.

Through the works of classic authors, Emily discovered a tapestry of human emotions and experiences that resonated deeply with her own. She explored the complexities of human nature, the depths of despair, and the capacity for redemption. The characters she encountered became her companions, their stories interwoven with her own.

In the tragedy of Shakespearean plays, Emily found echoes of her own struggles. She witnessed the tormented souls of Hamlet and Macbeth, grappling with their inner demons and the consequences of their actions. These characters served as cautionary tales, reminding her of the destructive paths that addiction could lead to if left unchecked.

Emily discovered solace in the pages of Jane Austen's novels, where she encountered heroines navigating the challenges of society, love, and self-discovery. She saw herself reflected in the struggles of Elizabeth Bennet in "Pride and Prejudice," as she confronted societal expectations and grappled with her own personal growth. Through Austen's works, Emily gained insights into the power of self-reflection, the importance of authenticity, and the pursuit of true happiness.

In the works of Fyodor Dostoevsky, Emily delved into the depths of human psyche and existential questions. The characters in "Crime and Punishment" and "The Brothers Karamazov" wrestled with their own inner demons and grappled with moral dilemmas. Through their journeys, Emily explored the intricacies of guilt, remorse, and the potential for redemption.

Emily's journey also intersected with the writings of Hermann Hesse, who explored themes of self-discovery and the search for meaning. In "Siddhartha" and "Steppenwolf," she found characters on transformative journeys of self-realization and enlightenment. Their quests for inner peace and understanding mirrored her own pursuit of healing and self-discovery.

As Emily immersed herself in the classics, she realized that the struggles of these fictional characters mirrored the complexities of her own life. Their stories provided her with perspectives, insights, and lessons that resonated deeply within her soul. She drew strength from their resilience, their capacity for growth, and their ultimate triumphs over adversity.

Through the timeless wisdom of classic literature, Emily discovered that her own journey was not isolated or unique. She recognized the universality of human experiences and the power of storytelling to illuminate the human condition. The struggles and triumphs of fictional characters became beacons of hope, guiding her towards her own transformation.

In the quiet moments spent with these literary treasures, Emily found solace and inspiration. She took refuge in the depths of prose and poetry, finding comfort in the beauty of language and the resonance of profound truths. The classics became her mentors, offering her wisdom, guidance, and a sense of belonging in the vast tapestry of human experiences.

Armed with the lessons learned from the classics, Emily navigated the complexities of her own journey with newfound resilience and determination. She understood that her story was part of a larger narrative, an interconnected web of human existence where struggles and triumphs intertwined.

The lessons from the classics fueled Emily's inner fire, propelling her forward on her quest for healing, self-discovery, and personal growth. Their timeless wisdom became a compass, guiding her towards the light of self-realization and the embrace of her own authentic voice.

As Emily continued to draw solace and guidance from the classics, she realized that the power of literature transcended time and space. The words of these authors, written centuries ago, still resonated with the deepest corners of her soul. In their stories, she found a roadmap for her own transformation, a testament to the enduring power of storytelling and the human capacity for resilience and redemption.

In her quest for healing and self-discovery, Emily ventured into the realm of art, discovering its transformative power as a means of self-expression and healing. Through various artistic mediums, she embarked on a journey of exploration, using art as a tool to navigate her emotions, confront her past, and find solace in the creative process.

Emily found herself drawn to the canvas, the blank surface awaiting her brushstrokes. As she dipped her brush into vibrant colors, she discovered a new language—a visual expression of her innermost thoughts and feelings. With each stroke, she released the emotions that had been confined within, allowing them to manifest into shapes and colors on the canvas.

Art became a sanctuary, a space where Emily could communicate without words, where she could give form to the intangible. Through her paintings, she found catharsis—a release of pent-up emotions and a gateway to self-understanding. The process of creating art became a form of therapy, a way to explore her inner landscape and bring forth the hidden aspects of her journey.

In addition to painting, Emily experimented with other artistic mediums. She immersed herself in the world of sculpture, molding clay with her hands and shaping it into meaningful forms. The tactile nature of sculpting allowed her to connect with her emotions on a deeper level, as she transformed shapeless clay into tangible representations of her experiences.

Dance became another avenue for self-expression and healing. Emily lost herself in the graceful movements of her body, using dance as a language to convey her emotions. With each twist, turn, and leap, she found liberation—a release from the shackles of her addiction and a celebration of her newfound freedom.

Writing poetry became an intimate dialogue with her

inner self. Through the rhythmic flow of words, Emily explored the depths of her emotions, capturing the essence of her journey in verses that danced on the page. Poetry became a bridge between her thoughts and her heart, a medium through which she could distill her experiences into poignant expressions of truth.

As Emily delved deeper into the world of art therapy, she discovered that the act of creation held immense transformative potential. Art became a mirror, reflecting her inner landscape and allowing her to explore the depths of her being. It provided her with a safe space to confront her past, heal emotional wounds, and embark on a path of self-discovery.

Through art, Emily found a sense of empowerment. She realized that she had the ability to shape her own narrative, to redefine herself through the creative process. Each stroke of the brush, each movement of her body, and each carefully chosen word became an act of self-affirmation—a declaration of her resilience and her capacity for growth.

Art also became a bridge between Emily and others who had experienced similar struggles. Through her creations, she connected with a community of individuals who found solace and healing in artistic expression. The shared language of art transcended barriers and offered a sense of belonging and understanding.

As Emily continued to explore the healing power of art, she discovered that the creative process itself was a transformative journey. It was not just about the final product, but about the introspection, self-discovery, and growth that unfolded along the way. Art became a companion on her path, a constant source of inspiration, and a powerful tool for healing.

In the realm of art, Emily found the freedom to express herself authentically, to peel back the layers of her identity and embrace her true essence. Through painting, sculpting, dancing, and writing, she unleashed her creativity, allowing her inner voice to be heard and celebrated.

Art became a beacon of light, illuminating the darkest corners of her journey and guiding her towards a renewed sense of self. Through the transformative power of artistic expression, Emily began to heal, to rediscover her inner strength, and to embrace the beauty of her own uniqueness.

With each brushstroke, each movement, and each word, Emily's artistic journey mirrored her own journey of healing and self-discovery. The transformative potential of art therapy unfolded before her eyes, as she witnessed the profound impact it had on her well-being and her ability to navigate the complexities of her own story.

Through art, Emily found liberation, healing, and a renewed sense of purpose. It became her sanctuary, her refuge, and her catalyst for growth. In the colorful palette of her artistic creations, she discovered the transformative power of self-expression, reminding herself that she was more than her past, more than her addiction—she was an artist, a creator, and a survivor.

As Emily ventured further along her path of healing and self-discovery, she encountered an unexpected mentor—a figure who would provide guidance, support, and encouragement throughout her transformative journey. This mentor's presence would prove instrumental in helping Emily navigate the twists and turns of her quest, offering wisdom, insight, and a steadfast belief in her potential.

It was during a chance encounter at a local art gallery that Emily first crossed paths with the mentor figure. She was captivated by a particular painting, her eyes drawn to the vibrant colors and the raw emotion captured on the canvas. As she stood there, lost in contemplation, a kind voice broke the silence.

"Beautiful, isn't it?" the voice said.

Emily turned to find a gentle-faced woman with wise eyes and a warm smile. There was an aura of calm and wisdom that radiated from her, drawing Emily in.

"Yes, it is," Emily replied, her voice filled with awe.

They began to engage in a conversation that flowed effortlessly, as if they were old friends reconnecting after a long separation. The woman, named Sophia, shared her own journey of healing and self-discovery through art, recounting how it had transformed her life in profound ways.

Sophia became Emily's guiding light, a mentor who understood the complexities of her journey and offered a compassionate ear and a wealth of wisdom. Through their conversations, Sophia gently encouraged Emily to embrace her own unique voice, to trust in her intuition, and to have faith in her ability to overcome the challenges that lay ahead.

Under Sophia's mentorship, Emily learned to look inward, to listen to her inner whispers, and to trust her own instincts. Sophia guided her through moments of self-doubt, reminding her that healing and self-discovery were not linear processes, but rather a series of small steps and profound realizations.

Sophia introduced Emily to new perspectives, challenging

her to question her preconceived notions and to see the world through different lenses. They delved into deep conversations about the nature of addiction, the complexities of the human psyche, and the transformative power of self-compassion.

But it wasn't just in their discussions that Sophia's guidance was evident. She also led by example, demonstrating resilience, authenticity, and a genuine love for life. Sophia's own artistic creations served as a testament to the power of self-expression and the beauty that could emerge from embracing one's inner truth.

Together, they embarked on various creative endeavors —painting, writing, and even collaborating on a joint art project. Through these shared experiences, Emily not only honed her artistic skills but also discovered the joy of collaboration and the power of creative synergy.

Sophia became Emily's pillar of support, encouraging her to persevere in the face of challenges and setbacks. When doubt crept in, Sophia would gently remind her of the progress she had already made and of the strength that resided within her.

Through Sophia's mentorship, Emily learned that the journey of self-discovery was not meant to be traversed alone. Sophia provided a safe space for Emily to share her deepest fears, her vulnerabilities, and her triumphs. With unwavering support and genuine empathy, Sophia offered a constant reminder that she was not alone on this transformative journey.

As time passed, Emily's bond with Sophia deepened, evolving into a lifelong friendship rooted in shared experiences, mutual growth, and an unbreakable bond forged through their respective journeys of healing and self-discovery.

With Sophia by her side, Emily felt a renewed sense of purpose and a belief in her own potential. Through Sophia's guidance, she learned that healing was not about erasing the past but rather about embracing all facets of her story—the broken pieces, the triumphs, and the moments of self-realization.

In Sophia, Emily had found a mentor, a confidante, and a guiding light who illuminated the path ahead. Sophia's presence in her life was a constant reminder that healing was possible, that self-discovery was a lifelong journey, and that Emily possessed the strength and resilience to create the life she desired.

As Emily continued on her path, guided by the wisdom of her mentor, she held onto the lessons learned, the newfound strength gained, and the unwavering belief in her own potential. Sophia's influence would forever be etched in her heart, a reminder of the transformative power of human connection and the profound impact a mentor can have on one's journey of self-discovery.

Throughout her journey of healing and self-discovery, Emily had been confronted with moments of vulnerability—moments when she felt exposed, raw, and uncertain. At first, she had seen vulnerability as a weakness, something to be avoided and hidden away. But as she continued on her path, guided by her experiences and the wisdom she had gained, Emily began to understand that vulnerability was not a flaw to be concealed but rather a profound source of strength and transformation.

It was during a group therapy session that Emily had her breakthrough. Surrounded by others who had their own struggles and stories to share, she found herself opening up, baring her soul, and exposing her deepest fears and insecurities. The act of vulnerability felt uncomfortable and unfamiliar, but as she spoke her truth, she noticed a shift within herself—a sense of liberation, a release from the weight she had been carrying.

In that moment, Emily realized that vulnerability was not a sign of weakness but an act of courage. It was through vulnerability that she could confront her fears, acknowledge her pain, and lay the foundation for true healing and self-discovery.

With this newfound perspective, Emily began to embrace vulnerability in all aspects of her life. She allowed herself to be seen, to express her emotions, and to share her struggles without shame or judgment. In doing so, she discovered a profound sense of connection and authenticity—a deepening of relationships built on genuine understanding and compassion.

Emily found that when she embraced vulnerability, others responded with empathy and support. By opening up about her journey, she created a safe space for others to do the same. The walls that had once isolated her from the world began to crumble, replaced by bridges of understanding and shared experiences.

Embracing vulnerability also allowed Emily to delve deeper into her own self-discovery. She realized that by being vulnerable, she could access the hidden depths of her emotions and beliefs. She explored her past with a newfound curiosity, unearthing buried memories and unraveling the tangled threads of her addiction.

Through vulnerability, Emily found the courage to confront her own shortcomings and take responsibility for her actions. She acknowledged the pain she had caused herself and others, and with that acknowledgment came the opportunity for growth and forgiveness.

As she embraced vulnerability, Emily discovered that it was not a one-time act but a continuous practice—a daily choice to lean into discomfort, to peel back the layers of protection, and to allow her true self to be seen and heard. She learned to sit with her own discomfort, to embrace the messy and imperfect parts of her journey, and to trust in the process of healing.

With vulnerability as her ally, Emily began to redefine her relationship with herself and the world around her. She let go of the need for control and perfection, embracing the beauty of imperfection and the richness of human connection. Vulnerability became a guiding principle, a compass that led her towards authenticity, self-compassion, and a deeper understanding of her own worth.

Through embracing vulnerability, Emily discovered that true healing was not about erasing the past or escaping the pain but about leaning into it, feeling it, and allowing it to transform her. It was through vulnerability that she found the strength to confront her inner demons, to rewrite her story, and to step into a future filled with possibility and self-discovery.

As Emily continued on her journey, she carried the lessons of vulnerability with her, embracing each new challenge and opportunity with an open heart and a willingness to be seen. She knew that true healing and self-discovery required her to be brave, to show up authentically, and to embrace the vulnerability that had become her greatest strength.

4

A Stranger's Embrace

Emily found herself drawn to the depths of her own psyche, seeking solace in the exploration of her inner landscape. It was during one of her contemplative walks through a tranquil park that fate intervened, leading her to a chance encounter that would forever alter the course of her journey.

The day was bathed in golden sunlight, casting a warm glow over the lush greenery that surrounded Emily. As she meandered along the winding paths, lost in her own thoughts, her attention was unexpectedly captivated by a man seated on a park bench. His demeanor exuded a sense of serenity and wisdom, as if he held the answers to life's most profound questions.

Curiosity piqued, Emily approached the enigmatic figure, feeling an unspoken connection that seemed to transcend the boundaries of time and space. As their eyes met, she sensed an instant recognition, as if they had known each other in some distant realm. The man's name was Ethan, and he emanated an aura of calmness that enveloped Emily like a soothing balm.

Their conversation flowed effortlessly, as if they were old friends who had been separated by the currents of life. Ethan possessed a deep understanding of addiction and the intricacies of the healing process, sharing his own journey of overcoming personal struggles and finding meaning in the midst of chaos.

It became evident to Emily that Ethan was no ordinary stranger; he was a healer—an individual who had dedicated his life to guiding others through the labyrinth of their own pain and self-discovery. His words were imbued with wisdom and empathy, resonating deep within Emily's soul and striking a chord of recognition.

As they spoke, Ethan unveiled his own experiences with addiction—a harrowing journey that mirrored Emily's own. He spoke of the dark depths he had descended to, the battles he had fought, and the profound transformation that had emerged from the ashes of his past. It was as if his words were a mirror, reflecting back to Emily her own struggles, fears, and aspirations.

Through their conversations, Ethan unveiled the underlying patterns and root causes that fueled addiction—the unhealed wounds, the yearning for connection, and the search for a sense of purpose. He imparted invaluable insights into the healing process, urging Emily to approach her journey with compassion, self-acceptance, and an unwavering belief in her own capacity for change.

In Ethan's presence, Emily felt a sense of safety and

understanding she had never experienced before. He saw beyond the surface of her addiction, delving into the depths of her soul with an uncanny ability to uncover the hidden truths and unspoken longings that lay dormant within her.

Together, they embarked on a profound exploration of the self—a journey that transcended traditional boundaries and ventured into the realm of the soul. They delved into the intricate tapestry of emotions, memories, and beliefs that had shaped Emily's addiction, unraveling the threads that held her captive and uncovering the transformative power of self-awareness.

Ethan introduced Emily to various healing modalities, each tailored to address a specific aspect of her journey. They delved into mindfulness practices, cultivating present-moment awareness and the ability to observe her thoughts and emotions without judgment. They explored the power of somatic healing, tapping into the wisdom of the body to release stored trauma and reestablish a sense of safety and grounding.

Under Ethan's guidance, Emily learned the art of radical self-compassion—a gentle embrace of her own imperfections and a commitment to treating herself with kindness and understanding. She discovered that healing was not a linear path but a continuous cycle of growth and self-reflection, each step forward accompanied by moments of struggle and surrender.

As their connection deepened, Ethan became more than a mentor to Emily; he became a confidante, a guide, and a catalyst for transformation. Their encounters were marked by a sense of profound resonance, as if they were dancing to the same rhythm of the universe, united in their shared pursuit of healing and self-discovery.

Together, they explored the labyrinth of emotions—grief, anger, fear, and joy—unraveling the layers that had kept Emily trapped in the cycle of addiction. Ethan encouraged her to face her fears head-on, to embrace the discomfort, and to trust in her own resilience. He reminded her that healing required the courage to confront the shadows, to unearth the buried pain, and to integrate the fragmented parts of herself.

Through Ethan's guidance, Emily began to recognize her own inherent worth and the immense potential that lay dormant within her. He encouraged her to nurture her passions, to cultivate self-expression, and to honor her unique gifts. With his support, she discovered the transformative power of creativity as a vehicle for self-discovery and healing.

Their encounters became a sanctuary for Emily—a sacred space where vulnerability was met with compassion, where her darkest secrets were held with reverence, and where the wounds of the past were met with the light of understanding. In Ethan's presence, she felt seen, heard, and accepted—a testament to the healing power of authentic connection.

As Emily continued her journey under Ethan's gentle guidance, she began to realize that their encounter was not a mere coincidence but a serendipitous intersection of two souls destined to cross paths. Ethan had been a catalyst—a guiding light in her darkest moments, illuminating the path towards wholeness and self-empowerment.

Their time together was not indefinite; eventually, their paths diverged, leaving Emily with a heart filled with gratitude and a renewed sense of purpose. But the imprint Ethan had left on her soul was indelible—a reminder that healing can be found in the most unexpected places and that the universe has a way of aligning the right people at the right time.

As Emily bid farewell to Ethan, she carried his wisdom and guidance in her heart, empowered to continue her journey of healing and self-discovery. The encounter with this enigmatic healer had transformed her perception of herself and the world around her, instilling within her a sense of hope, resilience, and an unwavering belief in the inherent capacity for change.

From that day forward, Emily embraced the lessons she had learned from Ethan, infusing them into her daily life. She approached each moment with curiosity, compassion, and a willingness to embrace the unknown. With Ethan's teachings as her compass, she set forth on her path with renewed determination, ready to face the challenges ahead and embrace the transformative power of healing and self-discovery.

And as she ventured forward, guided by the echoes of Ethan's wisdom, Emily discovered that within her own being lay the keys to her liberation—a liberation that would not only heal her wounds but also illuminate the path for others who sought solace and transformation on their own journeys of healing and self-discovery.

As the days turned into weeks and weeks into months, Emily and Ethan's connection deepened through their soulful conversations. They sat together in quiet corners of coffee shops, strolled through parks enveloped in nature's embrace, and found solace in the comfort of Ethan's cozy living room. Their conversations became a sacred space where vulnerability was welcomed, and the depths of their souls were laid bare.

One evening, as the sun cast a warm golden hue over the horizon, Emily found herself sharing the struggles she had faced throughout her addiction journey. Tears welled in her eyes as she spoke of the moments of despair, the battles with self-doubt, and the fear of relapse that haunted her. Ethan listened intently, his eyes filled with compassion, and he responded with words that would forever resonate within Emily's heart.

"Erika, addiction is not a mark of weakness; it is a reflection of the human condition. We all have our own battles, our own demons to face. What matters is not the fall, but the strength to rise again, to acknowledge our pain, and to seek the path of healing."

His words echoed through Emily's being, soothing her wounded soul and granting her the permission to be gentle with herself. In that moment, she realized that she was not alone in her struggles, that the weight she carried could be lightened through shared understanding and compassion.

On another occasion, as the moon cast its silvery glow over the world, Emily confessed her fear of relapse—a fear that lingered like a shadow even as she took steps towards healing. Ethan's voice resonated with wisdom as he responded, "Emily, fear is a natural companion on this journey. But remember, you are not defined by your past, nor are you destined to repeat it. Each day is an opportunity to make choices that align with your deepest desires and aspirations. Trust yourself, trust the process, and have faith in the strength you have cultivated."

His words ignited a spark of hope within Emily, reminding her that she possessed the power to shape her own destiny, that she was not bound by the chains of her past. Through their conversations, Ethan became her anchor, guiding her through the stormy waters of uncertainty and gently nudging her towards self-belief.

In the midst of a rain-soaked afternoon, Emily shared with Ethan her longing for a sense of purpose—a yearning to find meaning in her life beyond the confines of her addiction. With a gentle smile, Ethan leaned forward and spoke words that resonated deep within her soul.

"Emily, purpose is not a destination but a journey. It is found in the small moments of connection, in the acts of kindness and compassion that ripple through the world. Your experiences have given you a unique perspective, a depth of understanding that can be a guiding light for others who are still searching for their own path. Embrace your journey of healing, and let your purpose unfold naturally."

His words sparked a flame of inspiration within Emily. She began to see her journey not as a burden to bear but as a tapestry of experiences that could be woven into something meaningful, something that could bring light and healing to others who walked a similar path.

Their conversations delved into the depths of addiction, healing, and self-discovery, but they also explored the vast landscape of life's profound questions. They contemplated the nature of human existence, the meaning of suffering, and the beauty of resilience. Their souls danced in the realm of possibility, fueled by the exchange of ideas, the sharing of personal stories, and the mutual support they provided.

Through their conversations, Emily and Ethan discovered that their experiences, though unique, held remarkable parallels. They saw reflections of their own struggles and triumphs in each other's stories, creating a bond that transcended words alone. They became pillars of strength for one another, offering solace, encouragement, and a safe space to express their deepest fears and aspirations.

As Emily's journey continued, their conversations remained a source of nourishment for her soul. They served as a reminder that healing was not a solitary pursuit but a shared exploration, and that through the power of authentic connection and understanding, true transformation could be achieved.

Their conversations were a testament to the power of vulnerability, empathy, and the human spirit's capacity for growth. Through the exchange of their stories and experiences, Emily and Ethan not only found solace in each other's presence but also discovered the transformative power of genuine connection—a power that had the potential to ignite healing, awaken dormant potential, and pave the way for a brighter, more fulfilling future.

In the tapestry of their conversations, Emily and Ethan wove a profound bond—one that would forever remain etched in their hearts as a testament to the resilience of the human spirit and the infinite possibilities that lie within the realm of authentic connection.

As Emily and Ethan's connection deepened, so too did their willingness to confront the shadows that lurked within their pasts. They created a safe haven where vulnerability was met with compassion, and the wounds of their souls were tenderly tended to. Together, they embarked on a courageous journey of facing their darkest secrets and traumas, offering each other unwavering support and understanding along the way.

One moonlit evening, Emily mustered the courage to share a deeply guarded secret, her voice trembling with vulnerability. She spoke of a painful childhood marked by neglect and emotional turmoil—a childhood that had contributed to her addiction. The weight of her words hung heavy in the air as tears streamed down her face.

Ethan listened intently, his eyes reflecting the depths of empathy and understanding. With a gentle touch, he reassured Emily that she was not defined by her past, that her worth extended far beyond the traumas she had endured. He encouraged her to release the shame she carried, reminding her that healing began with acknowledging the wounds and offering herself the compassion she deserved.

Moved by Emily's bravery, Ethan reciprocated by sharing his own hidden pain, revealing the haunting memories that had shaped his own battle with addiction. The room seemed to hold its breath as he unveiled the layers of his past—a childhood marked by loss, a struggle for acceptance, and the scars left by unhealed wounds. Their shared vulnerability became a lifeline, intertwining their stories in a tapestry of understanding and mutual support.

Together, they confronted the shadows of their pasts, exploring the complex emotions that had been buried deep within their souls. They spoke of guilt, shame, and the remnants of self-destructive patterns that lingered even as they sought healing. Through their conversations, they peeled back the layers of pain, exposing the raw vulnerabilities that lay dormant within them.

In the safety of their shared space, Emily and Ethan learned to hold each other's pain with tenderness and compassion. They acknowledged that healing required time, patience, and a willingness to face the uncomfortable truths that had long been avoided. They became each other's allies, offering solace and understanding as they navigated the labyrinth of their darkest secrets and traumas.

Their shared journey through the shadows of their pasts became a testament to the resilience of the human spirit. It was within those depths of darkness that they discovered the seeds of their own strength and resilience, finding solace in the knowledge that they were not alone in their struggles.

Through their unwavering support, Emily and Ethan learned to rewrite the narratives that had defined them. They redefined their self-worth, recognizing that their pasts did not dictate their futures. In their shared vulnerability, they found the courage to let go of the shackles of shame, allowing themselves to be seen and embraced in their entirety.

As they navigated the shadows together, Emily and Ethan discovered the transformative power of compassion and empathy. They learned to hold space for one another's pain without judgment, cultivating an environment where healing could thrive. Through their shared vulnerability, they created a sanctuary—a place where the wounds of the past could be acknowledged, healed, and ultimately transformed into sources of wisdom and resilience.

In the depths of their conversations, they discovered that the journey of healing was not linear. It ebbed and flowed, filled with moments of triumph and moments of setback. But they held steadfast in their commitment to one another, knowing that together they could navigate the shadows and emerge stronger on the other side.

Their shared exploration of the depths of darkness became a testament to the power of genuine connection—a connection that provided the solace, understanding, and strength needed to confront the traumas that had haunted them. Emily and Ethan became beacons of light for one another, guiding each other through the labyrinth of their pasts, and ultimately, toward a future illuminated by the healing power of shared vulnerability and deep empathy.

In the realm of their connection, Emily and Ethan embarked on a profound journey of shared healing. United by their common experiences and their unwavering support for one another, they became each other's pillars of strength, offering empathy, understanding, and encouragement as they navigated the intricate path of recovery.

Their journey was marked by the highs and lows that often accompany the process of healing. In moments of triumph, they celebrated each other's milestones, rejoicing in the small victories that signified progress and growth. Whether it was a day of sobriety, a newfound sense of self-awareness, or a breakthrough in therapy, Emily and Ethan were there to cheer each other on, nurturing a sense of camaraderie and resilience.

But their journey was not without its challenges. There were days when the weight of temptation felt unbearable, when the shadows of the past loomed large, threatening to derail their progress. In those moments, Emily and Ethan turned to each other, finding solace in their shared understanding and offering a steadying presence amidst the storm.

They reminded one another of the strength they had culti-vated, the resilience that resided within, and the importance of self-compassion on the path to healing.

Through their joint journey, they discovered the transfor-mative power of empathy. As they shared their stories, their struggles, and their triumphs, they created a tapestry of con-nection—a tapestry woven with threads of vulnerability and understanding. Their shared experiences became a testament to the human capacity for healing and growth, inspiring one another to continue moving forward, even in the face of adversity.

Together, they explored various avenues of healing, seek-ing out therapies, support groups, and holistic practices that resonated with their unique journeys. They engaged in mind-fulness exercises, finding solace in the present moment and developing a greater sense of self-awareness. They delved into the world of self-care, recognizing the importance of nurtur-ing their physical, mental, and emotional well-being. And through it all, they provided a steadfast presence for one an-other, reminding each other that they were not alone in their pursuit of healing.

In the depths of their shared healing, Emily and Ethan discovered the transformative power of mutual support. They lifted each other up when doubt crept in, offering words of encouragement and a listening ear when needed. Their con-nection became a safe harbor, a sanctuary where they could lay down their burdens and find respite from the storms of life.

As they navigated the ups and downs of recovery, they learned that healing was not a linear journey. It was messy, non-linear, and deeply personal. But they embraced the imperfections, the detours, and the setbacks, knowing that growth often arises from the most challenging moments.

In the embrace of their shared healing, Emily and Ethan forged a bond that transcended the limitations of their individual journeys. They became witnesses to each other's transformation, celebrating the resilience, courage, and vulnerability that they displayed along the way. Their connection served as a reminder that healing was not solely an individual endeavor, but a collective process that was enriched by the presence of kindred spirits who walked alongside them.

Through their shared journey of healing, Emily and Ethan became beacons of hope for one another, igniting a flame of resilience and self-discovery that would continue to guide them long after their paths diverged. Their connection became a testament to the power of compassion, empathy, and genuine human connection on the path to healing and self-discovery. And as they continued their respective journeys, they carried with them the lessons learned and the strength gained through their shared healing, forever grateful for the transformative impact they had on each other's lives.

In the crucible of their shared experiences, Emily and Ethan embarked on a journey that not only nurtured their individual healing but also gave rise to a profound bond of trust. Through their vulnerability, they discovered the transformative power of trust—a foundation upon which their healing journey would flourish.

As they opened up to one another, revealing their deepest fears, traumas, and insecurities, a sense of safety enveloped their connection. They recognized that trust was not earned overnight but was built through the consistent demonstration of authenticity, empathy, and reliability. Each shared revelation, met with compassionate understanding, further solidified the trust that began to take root between them.

Through their shared experiences, Emily and Ethan came to understand that trust was a reciprocal gift. As they witnessed one another's vulnerability and held space for each other's pain, they recognized the power of their connection. Trust became the cornerstone upon which they could lean, finding solace in the knowledge that they could share their darkest moments without judgment or betrayal.

In the sanctuary of their trust, Emily and Ethan found the courage to confront the demons that had haunted them for far too long. They ventured into the depths of their wounds, knowing that they were not alone in their struggles. With each step forward, trust illuminated their path, providing them with the strength and resilience to face the challenges that lay ahead.

Through their shared vulnerability and trust, they discovered that healing was not a solitary endeavor. It was a collective journey, where the presence of another soul who genuinely understood and accepted them could make all the difference. Their connection became a refuge from the storm, a space where healing could unfold and growth could blossom.

As trust deepened, Emily and Ethan began to lean on one another for support, both in moments of triumph and in times of hardship. They became each other's confidants, offering a safe haven for the expression of emotions, doubts, and aspirations. The weight of their shared burdens was lightened as they allowed themselves to be seen, known, and accepted in their entirety.

Trust also opened the door to accountability. Emily and Ethan held each other accountable for their actions and choices, gently challenging one another to strive for growth and embrace new possibilities. They became mirrors for each other, reflecting the progress they had made and encouraging continued self-reflection and transformation.

In the embrace of trust, Emily and Ethan discovered a profound sense of belonging. They realized that they no longer needed to face their battles alone. They had found a kindred spirit—a partner in healing who walked beside them, offering unwavering support and understanding. The trust they had nurtured became a lifeline, a reminder that they were not defined by their pasts but were capable of forging a new future.

As their journey continued, trust infused their interactions with a sense of safety, authenticity, and acceptance. It allowed them to explore the uncharted territories of their hearts, unearthing hidden dreams, passions, and potentials. They encouraged each other to step outside of their comfort zones, knowing that the trust they had cultivated would catch them if they stumbled.

Through their shared experiences and the birth of trust, Emily and Ethan discovered that healing was not a destination but a continuous process—a journey of self-discovery, growth, and transformation. Trust became the bedrock upon which their healing was built, providing the stability and support necessary to navigate the complexities of their paths.

In the embrace of trust, Emily and Ethan flourished. They

realized that their connection was not simply about healing their individual wounds but also about uplifting and inspiring one another. They celebrated each other's progress, drawing strength from the knowledge that they had a steadfast ally by their side.

Their bond of trust became a testament to the resilience of the human spirit and the transformative power of genuine connection. As they continued their healing journey, Emily and Ethan carried the gift of trust with them, forever grateful for the profound impact it had on their lives.

5

Shadows of the Past

Within the tapestry of their shared healing, Emily and Ethan delved deeper into their pasts, uncovering the echoes of trauma that reverberated through their lives. As they embarked on this exploration, they began to understand the profound interconnection between their past experiences and their present struggles.

Emily and Ethan realized that their paths had been shaped by the wounds they carried, scars etched upon their souls. They opened up about their childhoods, the moments of pain and loss that had left indelible imprints on their hearts. They shared stories of shattered innocence, fractured relationships, and the lasting impact of neglect and abuse.

Through their conversations, Emily and Ethan discovered the ways in which their traumas had influenced their patterns of behavior and coping mechanisms. They recognized the inherent vulnerability and rawness that came with confronting the shadows of their pasts. It was in this vulnerability, however, that they found the strength to confront the wounds that had held them captive for far too long.

As they journeyed further into the shadows of their pasts, Emily and Ethan developed a deeper understanding of themselves and each other. They realized that their struggles with addiction were not isolated incidents but manifestations of the pain they had carried within. Their traumas had acted as catalysts for their addictive behaviors, providing temporary relief from the overwhelming emotions and memories that haunted them.

In the shared exploration of their pasts, Emily and Ethan found solace in the knowledge that they were not alone. They recognized the power of empathy, as they witnessed the resilience and courage it took for each other to confront their demons. The interconnectedness of their experiences allowed them to hold space for one another, providing unwavering support and understanding.

Through their conversations, they began to unravel the intricate web that connected their past traumas to their present struggles. They discovered the triggers that sent them spiraling, the wounds that still required healing, and the unhealthy patterns that had perpetuated their addictive behaviors. Together, they navigated the tangled landscape of their pasts, shedding light on the darkness and gaining a deeper understanding of themselves.

In the process of uncovering the shadows of their pasts, Emily and Ethan began to rewrite their narratives. They realized that they were not defined by their traumas, but rather by their resilience, strength, and capacity for healing. They acknowledged the pain they had endured, but also embraced the potential for growth and transformation.

As they confronted the shadows, Emily and Ethan learned the importance of self-compassion. They recognized that healing was not a linear process, but a journey of ups and downs, breakthroughs and setbacks. They offered each other compassion and understanding, reminding one another that healing took time and patience.

In the shadows of their pasts, Emily and Ethan found the seeds of resilience and hope. They acknowledged the wounds that had shaped them but refused to be defined by them. Together, they nurtured a sense of empowerment, reclaiming their narratives and taking ownership of their healing journey.

Through their shared understanding and exploration of the shadows, Emily and Ethan began to unravel the layers of their identities. They discovered the strength that lay hidden beneath the pain, the resilience that had carried them through the darkest moments. In the midst of their vulnerability, they forged a path towards healing, armed with the knowledge that their pasts did not have to dictate their futures.

As they continued their journey, Emily and Ethan recognized that the shadows of the past would always be a part of them. However, they also understood that they had the power to shape their present and future. They carried the lessons learned from their past traumas, using them as catalysts for growth, compassion, and self-discovery.

In the shadows of their pasts, Emily and Ethan found the courage to rewrite their stories, reclaim their power, and embrace the transformative potential of healing. They walked hand in hand, navigating the complex terrain of their pasts, knowing that the shadows could never extinguish the light of their resilience and determination.

Within the intricate tapestry of their healing journey, both Emily and Ethan faced moments of relapse—a reminder that recovery was not a linear path but a complex, twisting road with unexpected turns. However, it was their resilience and the unwavering support they provided to one another that allowed them to learn from setbacks and persevere in their healing process.

For Emily, the allure of her addiction still held a powerful grip at times. Despite her best efforts, she found herself succumbing to old habits, feeling the weight of shame and disappointment. In these moments, self-doubt crept in, threatening to overshadow the progress she had made. But it was in the depths of these relapses that her resilience emerged, guiding her back to the path of healing.

Ethan, too, encountered his own moments of vulnerability, where the temptations of his past whispered seductively in his ear. The familiar cravings tugged at his resolve, and he found himself standing at the crossroads of relapse and recovery. Yet, it was his resilience and the lessons he had learned throughout his journey that allowed him to make a different choice—to reach out for support, to confront his triggers, and to recommit to his healing.

In the face of relapse, Emily and Ethan demonstrated an unwavering determination to learn from their setbacks. Rather than allowing these moments to define them, they embraced them as opportunities for growth and self-reflection. They engaged in honest conversations, exploring the underlying triggers and patterns that led to their relapses. Together, they unraveled the complexities of addiction and understood that relapse did not equate to failure but was a part of the healing process.

The mutual support they provided was a lifeline in times of relapse. Emily and Ethan created a safe space where they could openly share their struggles, fears, and vulnerabilities. They leaned on each other for strength and encouragement, reminding one another of their worthiness and resilience. Their shared experiences allowed them to empathize with one another, providing the validation and understanding needed to navigate the difficult terrain of relapse.

Through the power of their connection, Emily and Ethan discovered that resilience was not about avoiding setbacks but about bouncing back stronger after experiencing them. They cultivated a mindset of self-compassion, recognizing that recovery was a lifelong journey filled with ups and downs. Instead of dwelling on their relapses, they focused on the lessons learned, using them as stepping stones towards greater self-awareness and growth.

Relapse became a teacher, guiding them towards areas of their healing that required further attention. They identified the triggers, patterns, and underlying emotions that contributed to their addictive behaviors. With each setback, they gained a deeper understanding of themselves and their individual paths to recovery.

In their shared resilience, Emily and Ethan fostered a deep sense of accountability. They held each other gently but firmly, encouraging one another to stay committed to their healing. They celebrated small victories and milestones, recognizing the progress they had made. Through their unwavering support, they were able to reframe relapse as an opportunity for renewed dedication, rather than a reason for despair.

Their resilience extended beyond their individual journeys; it permeated their relationship as well. Emily and Ethan recognized that their shared healing was not solely reliant on their own efforts, but on their collective strength. They drew inspiration and support from one another, bolstering each other's resolve in times of doubt. Their resilience as individuals was amplified by the resilience they found within their connection.

As they continued on their healing journey, Emily and Ethan understood that relapse might always be a possibility. But armed with their resilience and mutual support, they faced the challenges with renewed determination and resilience. They embraced the ebb and flow of recovery, knowing that setbacks were not indicative of failure, but rather opportunities for growth, self-discovery, and a deeper understanding of the intricacies of their own healing process.

Together, they stood strong, ready to face whatever challenges lay ahead, secure in the knowledge that their resilience would carry them through.

Within the depths of their healing journey, Emily and Ethan confronted the patterns and behaviors that had perpetuated their addiction. With unwavering determination, they embarked on a transformative quest to break free from the shadows of the past and forge a new path towards lasting recovery.

They recognized that breaking the cycle required a deep examination of the underlying triggers, thought patterns, and beliefs that had kept them trapped in the vicious cycle of addiction. Together, they explored the intricate web of their behaviors, unraveling the ways in which their past traumas had influenced their choices and coping mechanisms.

Emily and Ethan dove headfirst into the introspective work, peeling back the layers of their experiences to reveal the root causes of their addictive behaviors. They unearthed the insecurities, fears, and unresolved emotions that had served as fertile ground for their addiction to take hold. It was a difficult journey, as they confronted painful memories and faced their own vulnerabilities with unwavering courage.

They learned to identify the triggers that had perpetuated their addiction, whether it be stress, emotional pain, or moments of uncertainty. By recognizing these triggers, they gained the power to disrupt the cycle and develop healthier coping mechanisms. Through therapy, support groups, and self-reflection, they acquired the tools necessary to navigate life's challenges without resorting to their destructive patterns.

Breaking the cycle also required a deep examination of their thought patterns and beliefs. Emily and Ethan discovered the negative self-talk, distorted perceptions, and limiting beliefs that had fueled their addictive behaviors. With newfound awareness, they challenged these beliefs and actively worked to reframe their thinking. They embraced self-compassion, replacing self-judgment with self-love, and recognized their inherent worthiness of a life free from the grips of addiction.

In their journey to break the cycle, Emily and Ethan found solace in their shared experiences. They realized that they were not alone in their struggles, and their mutual support became a powerful catalyst for change. They held each other accountable, gently guiding one another towards healthier choices and encouraging one another to stay committed to their recovery.

They also sought guidance from professionals and mentors who provided them with the necessary tools and strategies to break free from the patterns that had held them captive. They learned to cultivate a support network that extended beyond their own relationship, creating a community of individuals who understood their journey and could provide guidance and encouragement along the way.

As they progressed on their path of breaking the cycle, Emily and Ethan celebrated each victory, no matter how small. They recognized that change was a gradual process, and every step towards healing was worth acknowledging. They allowed themselves to celebrate the moments of triumph, using them as fuel to propel themselves forward.

Breaking the cycle was not without its challenges. They faced moments of doubt, temptation, and setbacks. However, armed with their newfound self-awareness, resilience, and support system, they remained committed to their recovery. They embraced the understanding that setbacks were not failures but opportunities for growth and learning.

With each passing day, Emily and Ethan became more adept at breaking the cycle. They recognized the power of their choices and the agency they had in shaping their own lives. They refused to be defined by their pasts, instead embracing the transformative potential of the present moment.

Together, they created new habits, nurturing their minds, bodies, and spirits with practices that promoted wellness and balance. They prioritized self-care, engaging in activities that brought them joy and fulfillment. They learned to trust themselves and their instincts, forging a path towards a life that was authentic and true to their inner selves.

Breaking the cycle was not a one-time accomplishment but an ongoing process—a commitment to their own growth and well-being. Emily and Ethan vowed to continue challenging themselves, nurturing their resilience, and celebrating the milestones along their journey. In doing so, they broke free from the shadows of the past, reclaiming their lives and embracing a future filled with hope, purpose, and freedom.

In their profound journey of healing and self-discovery, Emily and Ethan confronted the weighty presence of forgiveness. As they delved into the depths of their past traumas and the consequences of their addiction, they grappled with the need to forgive, both themselves and those who had contributed to their pain.

Forgiveness, they realized, was not a simple act but a complex and transformative process. It required them to navigate through layers of hurt, anger, and resentment, and to unearth the courage to release the burdens that had weighed them down. They understood that forgiveness was not about condoning or forgetting the past, but about freeing themselves from the shackles of bitterness and resentment, allowing space for healing and growth to take root.

For Emily, forgiving herself was a daunting task. The mistakes and regrets she carried felt like an indelible stain on her soul. But as she embarked on her journey, she realized that self-forgiveness was essential for her healing. She learned to embrace her imperfections, acknowledging that her addiction did not define her worth. Through therapy and self-reflection, she embarked on a path of self-compassion, learning to forgive herself for the pain she had caused herself and others.

Ethan, too, grappled with the need to forgive himself. He had carried the weight of guilt and shame for far too long, allowing it to poison his self-perception and perpetuate his cycle of addiction. As he dove deeper into his healing journey, he learned to extend the same compassion and understanding to himself that he offered to others. He recognized that forgiveness was not a weakness but a strength—a powerful act of self-love and acceptance.

In addition to self-forgiveness, Emily and Ethan confronted the challenging task of forgiving those who had contributed to their pain. They faced the ghosts of their past—parents, friends, partners—who had played a role in their downward spiral. Forgiveness did not come easily; it required them to confront the pain, anger, and betrayal that had festered within them.

Through therapy and introspection, Emily and Ethan began to untangle the complex emotions tied to their past relationships. They realized that forgiveness was not about absolving the actions of others but about releasing the emotional attachments that kept them bound. They understood that holding onto resentment and anger only perpetuated their own suffering.

Forgiveness became a powerful act of liberation. It allowed them to reclaim their power, no longer defined by the actions of others. As they forgave, they created space for healing and growth. They realized that forgiveness was not an event but a process, requiring patience, self-compassion, and a willingness to let go.

In their shared journey, Emily and Ethan discovered that forgiveness was not a one-time act but a continuous practice. It required them to revisit and revisit again, as layers of pain and hurt resurfaced. But with each act of forgiveness, they found greater peace and freedom. They learned that forgiveness was not a linear path but a dance between grace and acceptance.

As they embraced forgiveness, Emily and Ethan experienced a profound shift within themselves. They let go of the heavy burdens they had carried for so long, allowing space for healing and self-discovery. Forgiveness became a bridge that connected them to their authentic selves and to a future that was no longer defined by past wounds.

Through forgiveness, they found the strength to rebuild their lives on a foundation of compassion, empathy, and self-love. They understood that forgiveness was not only a gift they gave to others but also a gift they gave themselves—an essential step towards inner peace and the restoration of their own wholeness.

In the end, forgiveness became a source of liberation, allowing Emily and Ethan to move forward with hearts unburdened and souls renewed. They embraced the power of forgiveness as a transformative force, propelling them further along their path of healing and self-discovery.

As Emily and Ethan continued their journey of healing and self-discovery, they discovered the transformative power of empathy. Through their shared experiences of addiction, they developed a deep understanding of the struggles faced by those grappling with similar challenges. This newfound empathy ignited a flame within them—a burning desire to extend a compassionate hand to others in need.

They recognized that addiction was not an isolated battle but a widespread issue that affected countless individuals. They realized that their own healing was intrinsically connected to the well-being of others. With hearts filled with empathy, they sought to create a ripple effect of understanding and support, reaching out to those who were still caught in the grips of addiction.

Emily and Ethan immersed themselves in the lives and stories of others, listening without judgment and offering a safe space for vulnerability. They became advocates for change, advocating for destigmatization and raising awareness about addiction and mental health. Through their own narratives of struggle and triumph, they inspired others to seek help and embark on their own paths of healing.

They joined support groups and recovery communities, becoming beacons of hope for those who felt lost and alone. They shared their experiences openly, offering a listening ear, words of encouragement, and guidance to those who were just beginning their own journey towards recovery. They understood that empathy was not just about feeling compassion but also taking action to support others.

In their interactions with others, Emily and Ethan cultivated empathy by recognizing the shared humanity that connected them all. They acknowledged that addiction did not discriminate—it could affect anyone, regardless of their background, age, or circumstances. This understanding allowed them to meet others with empathy and compassion, offering a hand to lift them up from the depths of despair.

Through empathy, they learned to hold space for others' pain, offering understanding without judgment. They understood that addiction was often a manifestation of deep-seated trauma and unmet emotional needs. With empathy as their guide, they encouraged others to seek professional help, therapy, and the necessary resources for their own healing journey.

As Emily and Ethan extended empathy to others, they also experienced a deepened sense of self-compassion. They realized that their own struggles were not a source of shame but an opportunity for growth and self-discovery. They embraced their imperfections and acknowledged that healing was a lifelong process, rooted in self-acceptance and love.

Their empathy became a beacon of light in the darkness, illuminating the path for others to find their way towards recovery. They understood the importance of providing support and resources to those who were ready to embark on their own healing journey. Through their advocacy and acts of kindness, they aimed to break down the barriers that prevented individuals from seeking help and fostered a community of understanding and acceptance.

In the embrace of empathy, Emily and Ethan discovered that true healing went beyond their own personal transformation—it extended to the collective healing of humanity. They understood that by sharing their stories, extending empathy, and advocating for change, they had the power to create a more compassionate and supportive world for all those affected by addiction.

With hearts open and filled with empathy, Emily and Ethan walked side by side, offering hope, understanding, and a gentle reminder that no one was alone in their struggles. They had learned that empathy was not a finite resource—it grew stronger with each act of kindness and connection. And in this realization, they found fulfillment, purpose, and a deeper sense of interconnectedness with all of humanity.

6

The Art of Letting Go

Within the depths of her healing journey, Emily stumbled upon a profound realization—the therapeutic power of painting. As she sought various forms of artistic expression, she discovered that painting provided a unique and transformative outlet for her emotions, allowing her to externalize and process the intricate tapestry of feelings within her.

With each stroke of the brush, Emily found solace and liberation. She embraced the blank canvas as a metaphor for her own life, a space where she could freely explore the depths of her emotions without judgment or restraint. Through vibrant colors, bold lines, and subtle brushwork, she unleashed the torrent of emotions that had been suppressed for far too long.

In the act of painting, Emily discovered a language that transcended words—an avenue to communicate the inexpressible. She recognized that some emotions were too complex, too nuanced to be captured through traditional means of expression. But within the realm of painting, she found a realm where emotions could be given form and substance, where the abstract and the concrete merged into a harmonious dance.

The act of painting became a cathartic release, a way to channel her inner turmoil onto the canvas. With each brushstroke, she let go of the weight that had burdened her soul, allowing the colors to speak the words she couldn't utter. The canvas became her confidant, witnessing her tears, her anger, and her moments of profound joy.

As she delved deeper into the world of painting, Emily discovered that the process was as significant as the finished artwork. It was a meditative practice that demanded her full presence and attention. She learned to be gentle with herself, embracing imperfections and surrendering to the flow of creativity. Through painting, she found a refuge—a space where time stood still, and her essence merged with the colors and textures she applied.

Each painting became a visual diary, a reflection of her inner landscape. She explored themes of struggle, resilience, and transformation, allowing her emotions to guide the brush. Sometimes, the strokes were wild and chaotic, mirroring her moments of despair and uncertainty. Other times, they were gentle and serene, reflecting the peace and clarity she discovered along her journey.

In the process of painting, Emily unearthed buried memories, unresolved traumas, and hidden desires. She confronted her demons with courage, facing the shadows that had held her captive. As she painted, she discovered healing in unexpected places, finding beauty and hope within the very depths of her pain.

Through painting, Emily learned the art of letting go. She embraced impermanence, recognizing that each stroke was a fleeting moment captured in time. She discovered the freedom in releasing attachments to outcomes, embracing the process rather than fixating on the end result. The canvas became a metaphor for life—a reminder that growth and transformation were ongoing, and that beauty could emerge even from the most chaotic of experiences.

As Emily shared her paintings with others, she witnessed the profound impact her artwork had on those who encountered it. People resonated with the emotions woven into each brushstroke, finding solace and inspiration within the vibrant colors and intricate textures. Her paintings became a conduit for empathy, connecting her to others who had experienced similar struggles, and offering them a visual language to express their own emotions.

Through the art of letting go, Emily not only discovered her own healing but also became a catalyst for healing in others. She realized that her paintings had the power to evoke emotions, provoke introspection, and ignite conversations. She started organizing art exhibitions and workshops, creating spaces where others could explore their own healing journey through art.

In the realm of painting, Emily found liberation, self-expression, and a profound connection to her inner self. She embraced the therapeutic power of art, using it as a vehicle for healing and self-discovery. Through her paintings, she discovered the beauty that could emerge from the depths of her struggles and shared that beauty with the world, reminding others of the transformative power of letting go and embracing the creative spirit within.

Through her artwork, Emily embarked on a journey of self-confrontation and integration. The canvas became a mirror, reflecting the fragmented parts of herself and offering a space for exploration, healing, and self-discovery.

As Emily confronted her innermost struggles, she found solace in the act of translating her emotions and experiences onto the canvas. Each stroke of paint became a bridge between her conscious and subconscious mind, a means of bringing to light the parts of herself that had long been hidden or suppressed.

With courage and vulnerability, Emily delved into the depths of her being, unraveling the complexities of her emotions, fears, and desires. Through the medium of art, she confronted the fragmented parts of herself, acknowledging their existence and seeking to understand their origins.

The process of creating art became a transformative experience for Emily. It was a dialogue between her conscious and unconscious self, a dance of introspection and revelation. As she painted, she observed the layers of her own psyche unfolding, each brushstroke peeling back the layers of her conditioning and revealing the raw essence beneath.

Through her artwork, Emily confronted her deepest fears and insecurities. She explored themes of loss, abandonment, and self-doubt, allowing herself to sit with the discomfort and unravel its roots. The canvas became a safe space for her to express the tangled emotions that had plagued her for years, offering a cathartic release and an opportunity for healing.

In the process of creating, Emily discovered that art had the power to transform her pain into something meaningful and beautiful. As she channeled her struggles onto the canvas, she found a sense of empowerment and agency. The act of creating art allowed her to reclaim her narrative, to redefine herself beyond the limitations of her past experiences.

Through her artwork, Emily began to piece together the fragments of her identity. She recognized that her struggles did not define her but were merely aspects of her multifaceted self. Each painting became a puzzle piece, contributing to the larger picture of who she was and who she aspired to be.

As she immersed herself in the creative process, Emily experienced moments of profound insight and self-reflection. She noticed patterns emerging in her artwork, recurring symbols and motifs that held personal significance. These artistic expressions served as signposts, guiding her towards a deeper understanding of herself and her journey of healing.

Through the canvas as a mirror, Emily discovered the power of self-acceptance and self-compassion. She learned to embrace the fragmented parts of herself, to hold space for her imperfections and vulnerabilities. Each painting became an act of self-love, a testament to her resilience and her willingness to confront her own shadows.

As Emily's artwork evolved, she began to see the interconnectedness of her struggles and her healing journey. She realized that the fragmented parts of herself were not separate entities but interconnected threads, woven together to form the tapestry of her life. Each stroke of paint represented a step towards wholeness, an opportunity to integrate the disparate aspects of her being.

Through her art, Emily invited others to confront their own fragmented selves and embrace the process of self-discovery. She shared her vulnerability, her triumphs, and her setbacks, creating a space for others to find solace and connection. The canvas became a mirror for all who encountered her artwork, a reflection of their own struggles, hopes, and potential for healing.

In the transformative embrace of the canvas as a mirror, Emily not only confronted her innermost struggles but also rediscovered the beauty and resilience that resided within her. Through her art, she became an inspiration for others, reminding them that their own fragmented selves were worthy of love, acceptance, and integration.

Within the realm of art, Emily embarked on a journey of exploration and experimentation, discovering the profound symbolism of colors and techniques in her quest for healing and self-discovery. Each stroke of the brush became a metaphorical step on her path, as she explored the transformative power of the healing palette.

In her artistic journey, Emily realized that colors held immense significance, representing various emotions, energies, and states of being. With an open mind and a curious spirit, she began to explore the vast spectrum of hues, allowing them to guide her through the intricate landscapes of her inner world.

She started with warm tones like fiery reds and vibrant oranges, symbolizing the intensity of her emotions and the burning desire for change. These bold colors mirrored her determination to confront her addiction and embark on a journey of self-discovery. With each stroke, she infused her artwork with the fiery passion that fueled her transformation.

As Emily delved deeper into her exploration, she discovered the calming and soothing properties of cool blues and tranquil greens. These colors represented the healing aspects of her journey, evoking a sense of serenity and harmony. She used them to paint tranquil landscapes, symbolizing moments of inner peace and self-reflection.

In her search for self-discovery, Emily also explored the power of earthy tones. Rich browns and deep greens became the canvas for her exploration of roots and grounding. Through these colors, she sought to connect with her past, her heritage, and the foundational elements that shaped her identity. They served as a reminder of the strength and resilience that lay within her roots.

Emily's palette expanded further as she experimented with contrasting colors and techniques. She discovered that the interplay of light and dark, of vibrant and muted shades, could represent the complexities of her healing journey. The juxtaposition of vibrant reds against muted grays became an expression of her inner battles and the contrasting emotions she experienced.

Techniques played a significant role in Emily's artistic exploration. She experimented with different brushstrokes, from bold and energetic to delicate and subtle. Each stroke carried its own meaning and intention, allowing her to convey a range of emotions and experiences. The choice of technique became a way for Emily to express the ebb and flow of her healing journey, from moments of intensity and release to moments of gentleness and introspection.

Through the healing palette, Emily discovered that her artwork was not just a means of external expression but also a mirror of her internal landscape. Each color and technique carried a story, a chapter in her journey of healing and self-discovery. With each stroke of the brush, she brought her emotions and experiences to life, imbuing her artwork with the transformative energy of her healing process.

As Emily shared her artwork with others, she witnessed the profound impact it had on those who encountered it. The colors and techniques spoke to the universal human experience, evoking emotions and reflections in others that mirrored her own. Through her artwork, she created a visual language of healing, inviting others to embark on their own transformative journeys.

In the realm of the healing palette, Emily found liberation and self-expression. She discovered that each stroke of the brush was a powerful act of self-discovery, a tangible representation of her inner landscape. Through the exploration of colors and techniques, she embraced the transformative power of art, using it as a vehicle for healing, self-expression, and connection.

Emily's artwork became a testament to her journey, a visual narrative of her struggles, triumphs, and the ever-evolving nature of her self-discovery. In the palette of healing, she found a sacred space to explore her emotions, to unveil the layers of her being, and to celebrate the beauty and resilience that emerged from her healing process.

Through her art, Emily invited others to explore their own healing palettes, to embrace the transformative potential of colors and techniques as a means of self-expression and self-discovery. She became a beacon of inspiration, reminding others that within the strokes of a brush lies the power to heal, transform, and unveil the beauty that resides within each individual.

In her journey of healing and self-discovery, Emily stumbled upon a profound realization – art could transcend the limitations of words, becoming a language of its own. As she delved deeper into her artistic expression, she discovered that her artwork had the power to communicate her emotions and experiences in ways that words could not.

Through her artwork, Emily found a voice that bypassed the constraints of language. Colors, shapes, and textures became her vocabulary, allowing her to express the depths of her emotions and the complexities of her experiences. In this visual language, she discovered a freedom of expression that went beyond the boundaries of spoken or written words.

As Emily delved into her artistic process, she realized that art had the ability to tap into the subconscious, bypassing the analytical mind and speaking directly to the soul. Each brushstroke, each composition, carried a depth of meaning that resonated with her on a profound level. Through her artwork, she was able to communicate the nuances and subtleties of her emotions, unveiling the unspoken truths within.

The abstract nature of art allowed Emily to convey emotions and experiences that were difficult to articulate through traditional means. She found that she could express her pain, her joy, her longing, and her healing journey through the interplay of colors, the rhythm of lines, and the texture of her brushstrokes. Her artwork became a visual symphony of emotions, inviting others to connect with her experiences on a deeply personal level.

Art became a universal language that transcended cultural, linguistic, and societal barriers. Emily's artwork resonated with others, evoking emotions and reflections that were unique to each individual. In this way, her art created a bridge of understanding and empathy, forging connections between souls that words alone could not achieve.

Through her artwork, Emily discovered that she could communicate the unspoken, the intangible, and the deeply personal. She found solace in the fact that her art had the power to touch others, to elicit emotions and spark conversations that words alone could not. It became a vessel for collective healing, a medium through which shared experiences and universal truths could be expressed and acknowledged.

Art became a sanctuary for Emily, a sacred space where she could reveal her true self without fear of judgment or misunderstanding. In the act of creating, she felt a sense of liberation and authenticity that permeated her entire being. Her artwork became a mirror that reflected her inner world, a testament to her resilience, and a celebration of her journey.

As Emily shared her artwork with others, she witnessed the power of art as a language of connection. Viewers found solace, inspiration, and a sense of validation in her creations. They saw their own struggles and triumphs mirrored in her art, finding comfort in the realization that they were not alone in their experiences. Through her artwork, Emily fostered a sense of community and belonging, reminding others of the healing potential that lies within artistic expression.

In the realm of art as a language, Emily found a voice that

resonated deeply with her own soul and the souls of others. She embraced the transformative power of visual communication, allowing her artwork to transcend the boundaries of words and touch the hearts of those who encountered it. Through her artistic expression, she became a storyteller, sharing her journey of addiction, healing, and self-discovery in a way that transcended the limitations of language.

Art became her conduit for truth, a vehicle for healing, and a means of connection. In the language of art, Emily found liberation, authenticity, and a profound sense of purpose. She realized that her artwork had the capacity to inspire, to provoke thought, and to ignite the flame of self-discovery within others. And so, with each stroke of the brush, she continued to communicate her emotions, her experiences, and her transformative journey, inviting others to find their own voice in the universal language of art.

In the depths of her artistic exploration, Emily discovered a profound power within the act of release. Through her art, she found a way to let go of her pain and trauma, creating a space for healing and liberation. The canvas became a sanctuary where she could unravel the tangled threads of her past, allowing her emotions to flow freely and finding a sense of inner peace.

With each brushstroke, Emily released fragments of her pain onto the canvas. The act of painting became a cathartic process, allowing her to externalize and confront the depths of her emotions. As the colors mingled and danced on the canvas, she felt a weight being lifted from her soul, a sense of release that permeated every stroke.

Through her art, Emily found a means of translating her

pain into something tangible, something outside of herself. She transformed her anguish, her fears, and her traumas into vibrant expressions of color and form. The act of creation became an alchemical process, transmuting darkness into light, despair into hope.

As she painted, Emily tapped into the innate wisdom of her intuition. She allowed her subconscious to guide her, trusting the flow of her brush and the interplay of colors. In this intuitive dance, she discovered hidden symbols and metaphors that spoke to her healing journey. Each composition held a story, a narrative of her transformation, and the release of her inner burdens.

Through the act of release, Emily found liberation. She let go of the shackles that bound her to her past, embracing the freedom to express her truth without reservation. The canvas became a mirror that reflected her growth, her resilience, and her capacity for healing. As she let go of her pain, she made room for joy, for self-discovery, and for the beauty that lay hidden within her.

The liberation she experienced through her art extended beyond the confines of the studio. It permeated every aspect of her life, as she embraced a newfound sense of authenticity and self-acceptance. The act of release allowed her to shed the masks she had worn for so long, revealing her true essence to the world. She found the courage to be vulnerable, to share her story, and to connect with others on a profound level.

In the liberation of release, Emily discovered the power of forgiveness and self-compassion. As she painted, she forgave herself for the mistakes of her past, recognizing that they were a part of her journey but did not define her. She offered herself compassion for the wounds she carried, acknowledging that healing was a process that required patience and gentleness.

Through her art, Emily also learned to release the expectations and judgments of others. She embraced the freedom to create for herself, to express her truth without seeking validation or approval. The act of release became an affirmation of her worth, a declaration that her voice mattered and deserved to be heard.

As Emily shared her artwork with the world, she witnessed the transformative power of release in others. Viewers connected with her paintings, finding solace and resonance in the emotions conveyed. They, too, felt a sense of liberation as they allowed themselves to release their own pain and embrace the healing journey.

Through the liberation of release, Emily discovered a profound sense of inner peace. The act of creating art became a meditative practice, a way to center herself and find serenity amidst the chaos of life. She learned to surrender to the creative process, embracing the unknown and trusting in the transformative power of her art.

In the release of her pain and trauma, Emily found liberation. She discovered that her art was not just a means of self-expression but a pathway to healing and inner peace. With each stroke of the brush, she continued to let go, allowing her art to be a vessel of release, transformation, and profound liberation.

7

The Phoenix's Flight

In the depths of her journey, Emily awakened to a dormant force within her—a wellspring of inner strength that had long been overshadowed by the grip of addiction. As she delved into the labyrinth of her psyche, she unearthed the embers of resilience that lay dormant within her soul, waiting to be ignited.

Like a phoenix rising from the ashes, Emily embarked on a transformative journey of self-discovery, fueled by the fiery determination to reclaim her life. She recognized that true strength resided not in the absence of struggle, but in the courage to confront and overcome it. With each step forward, she shed the weight of her addiction, emerging stronger and more resilient than before.

Awakening her inner strength required a deep introspection and a willingness to confront her vulnerabilities. Emily delved into the shadows of her past, exploring the root causes of her addiction and the underlying wounds that fueled it. Through therapy, self-reflection, and a commitment to healing, she began to understand the intricate layers of her experiences and the sources of her strength.

Emily discovered that strength was not synonymous with invincibility, but rather with vulnerability and authenticity. She learned to embrace her flaws and imperfections, recognizing that they were not signs of weakness but reflections of her humanity. It was in her willingness to face her weaknesses and acknowledge her limitations that she found the power to transcend them.

As Emily navigated the challenges of her healing journey, she encountered moments of doubt and temptation. The allure of her addiction beckoned her, whispering promises of temporary relief and escape. Yet, with each temptation, she called upon her newfound strength, grounding herself in the unwavering resolve to overcome. She refused to be defined by her past, choosing instead to write a new narrative—one of resilience, growth, and self-empowerment.

Through the support of her loved ones, therapy, and support groups, Emily built a network of allies who encouraged her on her path to recovery. They became her pillars of strength, holding space for her struggles and celebrating her victories. Their unwavering belief in her potential served as a constant reminder that she was not alone in her journey.

As Emily faced the challenges of withdrawal and the emotional rollercoaster of recovery, she discovered that her inner strength was not a finite resource but an infinite wellspring within her. It was a force that grew with each hurdle overcome and each milestone achieved. She found solace in the knowledge that strength was not something external to be sought, but an inherent part of her being.

Emily's journey was not without setbacks. There were moments when her strength faltered, when she stumbled and fell. But in those moments, she learned the art of resilience—forging ahead despite adversity, picking herself up, and continuing on her path. She recognized that setbacks were not failures but opportunities for growth and learning.

Through her journey, Emily began to redefine her concept of strength. It was no longer about conquering others or suppressing her vulnerabilities. True strength lay in the courage to face her fears, to embrace her authentic self, and to live in alignment with her values. It was in her ability to show up for herself, to ask for help when needed, and to persist even in the face of adversity.

With each step forward, Emily felt the reawakening of her spirit. She discovered the power of self-compassion, learning to treat herself with kindness and understanding. She realized that she deserved love and forgiveness, and that her past did not define her worth. It was through this self-acceptance that her inner strength flourished, like a blooming flower breaking through the cracks of a hardened shell.

As she continued to cultivate her inner strength, Emily's newfound resilience extended beyond her own journey. She became a source of inspiration and support for others battling addiction, offering a guiding light to those navigating their own paths of recovery. Through her vulnerability and authenticity, she demonstrated that strength was not a solitary pursuit but a collective endeavor.

In the crucible of her journey, Emily learned that strength

was not an external force to be obtained but an inherent part of her being—a flame waiting to be ignited. Through the trials and triumphs, she embraced her inner phoenix, spreading her wings and soaring towards a future of healing, self-discovery, and boundless possibility. Her flight symbolized the resilience of the human spirit and the transformative power of embracing one's inner strength.

As Emily's journey continued, she carried with her the knowledge that her inner strength was a lifelong companion, a constant source of resilience and empowerment. With each passing day, she embraced her authentic self and lived with a renewed sense of purpose. The phoenix within her continued to rise, illuminating her path and reminding her of the infinite possibilities that awaited her.

Chapter 7 marked a turning point in Emily's journey—a pivotal moment where she fully embraced her inner strength and embarked on a trajectory of empowerment and self-discovery. The flame of her resilience burned brightly, lighting the way for her to transcend her past and embrace a future filled with hope, purpose, and the unwavering knowledge that she had the strength to overcome any challenge that lay ahead.

As Emily's healing journey progressed, she found herself standing at the precipice of self-discovery, ready to embrace her true identity. For too long, she had been weighed down by the labels and expectations imposed upon her by society, as well as those she had internalized. But now, in the glow of her healing and self-empowerment, she shed these burdens, freeing herself to explore and embrace her authentic self.

Emily realized that her addiction had masked her true

identity, numbing her to the depths of her being. It had served as a shield, protecting her from the pain and uncertainty of facing her authentic self. But as she embarked on her journey of healing, she understood that in order to truly transform and find lasting happiness, she needed to strip away the layers of pretense and embrace her true essence.

With courage as her guide, Emily embarked on a process of self-exploration. She delved into her passions, interests, and values, seeking to uncover the facets of her identity that had long been suppressed. She questioned societal expectations and norms, challenging the boxes she had been placed in. She allowed herself the freedom to dream, to envision a life that aligned with her true desires and aspirations.

In the midst of this exploration, Emily confronted her fears and insecurities. She realized that shedding the labels and expectations placed upon her meant confronting the discomfort of uncertainty. It meant facing the judgments and criticisms of others who were invested in keeping her confined within their own limited perceptions. But she was determined to break free, to embrace the authenticity that had been yearning to be unleashed.

As Emily embraced her true identity, she discovered a sense of liberation and empowerment. She realized that she no longer needed to mold herself to fit into societal molds or meet the expectations of others. She embraced her quirks, her passions, and her unique perspective on the world. In doing so, she found a sense of belonging within herself—a deep, unshakeable connection to her true essence.

Emily's journey of self-discovery also brought about a profound sense of self-acceptance. She learned to embrace all aspects of herself—the light and the shadows, the strengths and the vulnerabilities. She recognized that her past struggles did not define her, but were part of the tapestry that made her who she was. She embraced her imperfections, knowing that they were what made her human, and they were what made her beautifully unique.

As she stepped into her authentic self, Emily also discovered a renewed sense of purpose and meaning. She recognized that her experiences, her healing, and her newfound understanding of self could be a source of inspiration and support for others. She became an advocate for authenticity, encouraging others to shed the societal masks and embrace their true identities.

The process of embracing her true identity was not without challenges. Emily faced moments of self-doubt and vulnerability as she navigated the uncharted territory of her authentic self. However, she found solace in the support of her loved ones, her newfound community, and the wisdom she had gained on her journey. She drew strength from knowing that she was not alone in her quest for self-discovery.

As Emily fully embraced her true identity, she radiated a sense of self-assuredness and inner peace. She walked with a newfound grace and authenticity, unapologetically embracing all that she was. She let go of the need for external validation and allowed her inner compass to guide her.

Through embracing her true identity, Emily found a profound sense of liberation and fulfillment. She no longer lived in the shadows of others' expectations but forged her own path, guided by her passions, values, and the truth of her being. In doing so, she embodied the essence of her authentic self, radiating a light that inspired others to do the same.

Chapter 8 marked a transformative chapter in Emily's journey—a chapter of self-discovery, self-acceptance, and the joy of embracing her true identity. It was a reminder to all that our greatest power lies in being authentically and unapologetically ourselves, and that in doing so, we invite the world to embrace us for who we truly are.

As Emily continued her journey of healing and self-discovery, she found herself reconnecting with a long-lost part of herself—the part that was fueled by passion and creativity. The chains of addiction had stifled her innate talents and dimmed the fire of her passions, but now, as she embraced her true identity, she felt a surge of energy and excitement coursing through her veins.

Emily delved deep into the recesses of her soul, unearthing the passions and talents that had lain dormant for far too long. She remembered the joy she once felt when pursuing creative endeavors, the sense of fulfillment that came from expressing herself through various art forms. It was time to reclaim those parts of herself and reignite the flame of her creativity.

With a renewed sense of purpose, Emily delved into her artistic pursuits. She picked up a paintbrush and let her emotions flow onto the canvas, creating vibrant and evocative works of art that spoke to her innermost being. She danced with abandon, allowing her body to express itself freely, uninhibited by the judgments of others. She wrote, pouring her thoughts and feelings onto the pages of her journal, finding solace and clarity in the written word.

As Emily embraced her passions, she found that time stood still. Engrossed in her creative endeavors, she experienced a sense of flow—an effortless immersion in the present moment where her worries and troubles faded away. The act of creating became a form of therapy, a sanctuary where she could explore her emotions, celebrate her strengths, and confront her fears.

Emily's rediscovered passions became a source of inspiration and self-discovery. Through her creative pursuits, she unearthed layers of her identity that had long been concealed. Each brushstroke, each dance step, each word written revealed a piece of her true essence, reflecting back to her the beauty and depth of her being.

As she shared her creations with others, Emily discovered the power of her art to touch hearts and evoke emotions. Her paintings resonated with those who had also experienced the depths of addiction and the journey of healing. Her dance performances inspired others to move with authenticity and express their innermost desires. Her writing became a voice for those who struggled to find the words to articulate their own experiences.

Emily's passion not only brought her personal fulfillment but also became a catalyst for connection and community. She found herself surrounded by like-minded individuals who shared her love for the arts, forming a support network of fellow creatives who understood the transformative power of self-expression. They celebrated each other's successes, provided encouragement during moments of doubt, and served as a reminder that they were not alone in their artistic journeys.

Through unleashing her passion, Emily discovered that creativity was not just a frivolous pursuit but a vital part of her well-being. It was a pathway to self-discovery, a medium through which she could explore the depths of her emotions, confront her past, and envision her future. It brought her joy, fulfillment, and a deep sense of purpose.

Emily's journey of unleashing her passion was not without its challenges. She faced moments of self-doubt and creative blocks, but she persevered, knowing that her artistic expression was a reflection of her authentic self. She allowed herself to experiment, to take risks, and to embrace the imperfections that were inherent in the creative process. In doing so, she discovered that true artistic expression was not about perfection but about authenticity and self-discovery.

As Emily continued to unleash her passion, she realized that it was not limited to specific artistic endeavors. Passion infused every aspect of her life—her relationships, her work, her daily activities. It fueled her purpose and guided her choices. She lived with a sense of vibrancy and aliveness, embracing each day as an opportunity to create, to connect, and to leave a lasting impact on the world.

In the journey of unleashing her passion, Emily found a profound sense of self-expression, fulfillment, and purpose. She discovered that within her resided a wellspring of creativity, waiting to be tapped into and shared with the world. And as she let her passions guide her, she found herself living a life of authenticity, joy, and unbridled creative potential.

As Emily progressed on her journey of healing and self-discovery, she came to a pivotal realization—a realization that would transform her relationship with herself and pave the way for deeper healing. She understood that alongside the pursuit of self-improvement and growth, there was a fundamental need for self-compassion.

For far too long, Emily had been her harshest critic. She held herself to impossible standards, berating herself for every perceived flaw and mistake. The weight of self-judgment had weighed heavily on her, perpetuating a cycle of shame and self-destructive behavior. But now, she recognized that in order to heal and truly embrace her authentic self, she needed to cultivate self-compassion.

With gentle determination, Emily embarked on the path of self-compassion, treating herself with the same kindness and forgiveness she would extend to a loved one. She learned to recognize that she was human, flawed yet deserving of love and understanding. She embraced her imperfections as part of her unique journey, understanding that they did not define her worth.

Self-compassion became a daily practice for Emily. She learned to quiet her inner critic and replace it with a voice of kindness and encouragement. She acknowledged her emotions and experiences without judgment, allowing herself to feel and process them with compassion. She learned to give herself permission to rest, to prioritize self-care, and to set boundaries that honored her well-being.

In moments of self-doubt and vulnerability, Emily turned to self-compassion as a guiding light. She reminded herself that she was worthy of love and acceptance, just as she was in that present moment. She offered herself forgiveness for past mistakes and embraced the opportunity for growth and transformation. Through self-compassion, she found the courage to extend grace to herself and release the heavy burden of self-blame.

As Emily cultivated self-compassion, she discovered that it had a profound impact on her healing journey. It became a wellspring of strength and resilience, allowing her to navigate setbacks and challenges with greater ease. It became the foundation for her self-care practices, reminding her to nurture her mind, body, and spirit. And most importantly, it became the catalyst for self-love—a deep and unconditional love that accepted and embraced all aspects of herself.

Through self-compassion, Emily learned to be her own ally and advocate. She recognized that self-care was not selfish but essential for her well-being. She prioritized her needs and desires, honoring her boundaries and communicating them with clarity and kindness. She surrounded herself with people who uplifted and supported her, fostering relationships that reflected her newfound self-worth.

In cultivating self-compassion, Emily also became more compassionate towards others. She recognized that everyone carried their own burdens and struggles, and she approached them with empathy and understanding. Her journey of healing had opened her heart to the suffering of others, and she became a source of support and compassion for those in need.

The practice of self-compassion was not without its challenges. Emily still encountered moments of self-doubt and old patterns of self-criticism. But she met those moments with patience and gentle persistence, reminding herself that self-compassion was a journey, not a destination. She celebrated her progress, no matter how small, and learned to embrace the process of growth with open arms.

As Emily embraced self-compassion, she experienced a profound shift in her relationship with herself and the world around her. She felt a deep sense of inner peace and acceptance, knowing that she was deserving of love and compassion. She lived with a newfound sense of liberation, free from the shackles of self-judgment. And in cultivating self-compassion, she discovered that true healing and self-discovery were rooted in the soil of self-love.

As Emily stood at the precipice of her healing journey, she felt a surge of excitement and anticipation for what lay ahead. Her addiction was now a distant memory, and she had emerged from the depths of her struggles stronger and more resilient than ever before. With a newfound sense of freedom and possibility, she set her sights on new horizons, ready to embrace ventures that would push her beyond her comfort zone and lead to further self-discovery.

The first step in Emily's quest for new experiences was to identify her passions and curiosities. She allowed herself to dream without limitations, exploring the depths of her desires and interests. She felt a stirring within her, an eagerness to explore uncharted territories and uncover hidden talents. With courage as her guiding companion, she ventured into unexplored realms.

Emily's journey beyond her limits took her to unfamiliar places, both physically and metaphorically. She traveled to distant lands, immersing herself in different cultures and expanding her worldview. She engaged in activities that had always intrigued her but had previously seemed out of reach. She challenged herself to try new things, embracing the exhilaration of stepping into the unknown.

In pushing herself beyond her comfort zone, Emily discovered new facets of her being. She found strength in moments of vulnerability, discovering that true growth often lies just outside the realm of familiarity. She welcomed the discomfort of uncertainty as a sign that she was expanding her horizons and embracing the fullness of life. Each new experience became a catalyst for self-discovery and personal transformation.

As Emily ventured into uncharted territories, she encountered obstacles and faced her fears head-on. She stumbled, she fell, but she also learned to rise and persevere. Through these challenges, she discovered the depths of her resilience and the power of her determination. She realized that her past struggles had not defined her, but had shaped her into a person capable of overcoming any obstacle.

Along her journey of soaring beyond limits, Emily encountered inspiring individuals who became her guides and mentors. She connected with kindred spirits who had also embarked on journeys of self-discovery and personal growth. They shared stories of triumph and resilience, providing encouragement and support as Emily faced her own challenges. These connections deepened her sense of belonging and reinforced her belief in the transformative power of human connection.

As Emily soared beyond her limits, she discovered that the process of self-discovery was an ongoing journey. It was not confined to a single destination but rather a lifelong exploration of her true potential. With each new experience, she gained a deeper understanding of herself—her strengths, her passions, and her purpose. She embraced the fluidity of her identity, knowing that she was constantly evolving and growing.

Through her ventures beyond her limits, Emily experienced a profound sense of liberation. She broke free from the confines of her past, embracing a life of boundless possibilities. She learned to trust in her abilities and intuition, to believe in her dreams, and to have the courage to pursue them. With each step forward, she realized that the only limits that existed were the ones she imposed upon herself.

As Emily soared beyond her limits, she became a beacon of inspiration for others who were on their own paths of self-discovery. Her story served as a reminder that no matter how challenging the journey may be, there is always the potential for growth, transformation, and the realization of one's true potential.

And so, Emily continued to soar, embracing the vast expanse of the unknown with open arms and an unwavering spirit. With every new adventure, she discovered more about herself and the limitless possibilities that awaited her. She lived a life defined by curiosity, resilience, and the unwavering belief that she was capable of reaching heights she had once only dreamed of.

In soaring beyond her limits, Emily discovered that the sky was not the limit—it was only the beginning of her boundless potential.

8

A Fragile Euphoria

In the tapestry of Emily's healing journey, there were moments that shone with a brilliant light—a light that illuminated her path and affirmed the progress she had made on her road to recovery. These were the moments of triumph, the milestones she reached that served as beacons of hope and reminders of her strength.

Each milestone represented a step forward, a testament to Emily's resilience and unwavering commitment to her healing journey. They were the culmination of days, weeks, and months of hard work, self-reflection, and personal growth. As she looked back on these moments, she couldn't help but feel a surge of pride and gratitude for how far she had come.

One such moment of triumph came when Emily celebrated her first year of sobriety. It was a poignant occasion that marked a significant milestone in her recovery. She reflected on the challenges she had overcome, the temptations she had resisted, and the inner battles she had fought with un-wavering determination. It was a moment of immense pride, a testament to her courage and the power of her will.

Another moment of triumph emerged when Emily suc-cessfully completed a therapy program designed specifically for individuals on the path to recovery. The program provided her with valuable tools, support, and a safe space to explore the underlying causes of her addiction. It was a transforma-tive experience that allowed her to delve deep into her past, confront her demons, and develop healthier coping mecha-nisms. As she graduated from the program, she carried with her a newfound sense of self-awareness and a strengthened commitment to her ongoing healing.

There were also smaller moments of triumph scattered throughout Emily's journey. Moments when she resisted the pull of her addiction in the face of temptation. Moments when she chose self-care and self-compassion over self-destruction. Moments when she faced her fears and took steps towards her dreams. These seemingly ordinary moments held extraor-dinary significance, for they were evidence of the profound shifts happening within her.

Each triumph, big or small, carried a fragile euphoria—a delicate sense of joy that permeated Emily's being. It was a feeling that reminded her of her inherent worth and the limitless possibilities that lay before her. It was a gentle affirmation that she was capable of rewriting her story and reclaiming her life.

But alongside the euphoria, Emily also recognized the fragility of these moments. She understood that recovery was not a linear path but a complex, nuanced journey filled with ups and downs. The moments of triumph were not immune to the challenges and setbacks that she would inevitably encounter. They were delicate petals that could be easily bruised by the storms of life.

In embracing the fragility of her triumphs, Emily learned the importance of staying grounded and maintaining a sense of humility. She understood that true strength lay not in the absence of vulnerability, but in the courage to acknowledge it and seek support when needed. She surrounded herself with a supportive network of friends, family, and fellow travelers on the path of recovery, knowing that their presence would be invaluable during both moments of triumph and moments of struggle.

As Emily continued her journey, she cherished each moment of triumph as a precious gift. She celebrated them not only for herself but also for the countless others who were fighting their own battles and seeking their own moments of triumph. She became a source of inspiration and hope, sharing her story with authenticity and vulnerability, letting others know that recovery was possible, and that moments of triumph were within their reach.

Through the fragile euphoria of these moments, Emily discovered a deep appreciation for the beauty and complexity of her own journey. She understood that the triumphs were not the end goal, but rather meaningful signposts that guided her forward. They reminded her of her resilience, her capacity for growth, and the infinite potential that resided within her.

As the tapestry of Emily's healing journey unfolded, the moments of triumph woven into its fabric became beacons of light, guiding her through the darkest of times. They were reminders that no matter how difficult the road may be, there was always the possibility of finding joy, strength, and purpose along the way.

And so, Emily embraced the fragile euphoria of each triumph, cherishing them as milestones on her path to recovery. She walked forward with renewed determination, ready to face the challenges that lay ahead, knowing that with every step, she was becoming more resilient, more whole, and more alive.

As Emily basked in the glow of her triumphs and experienced moments of genuine happiness, she couldn't help but feel a sense of vulnerability. She understood that vulnerability was an integral part of the human experience, and it had played a significant role in both her addiction and her healing journey. Now, as she stood at the crossroads of her newfound happiness, she knew that navigating vulnerability with grace and resilience would be crucial in maintaining her progress.

Vulnerability was not an easy concept for Emily to embrace. It had often been the catalyst for her addiction, a vulnerability she sought to escape from rather than confront. But through her journey of self-discovery, she had come to realize that vulnerability was not a weakness but a strength. It was the gateway to authentic connections, personal growth, and a life filled with purpose and meaning.

With this newfound understanding, Emily began to navigate vulnerability with a sense of grace and resilience. She recognized that vulnerability was not something to be feared or avoided but rather something to be acknowledged and embraced. It was an opportunity to show up fully, to be seen and heard, and to forge deep connections with others.

In her relationships, Emily learned to communicate her needs and boundaries honestly and assertively, without fear of judgment or rejection. She understood that vulnerability required trust, both in herself and in others. By opening herself up and sharing her struggles, she allowed others to do the same, fostering an atmosphere of empathy and understanding.

Emily also learned to navigate vulnerability within herself. She acknowledged that healing was an ongoing process and that setbacks and challenges were a natural part of the journey. Instead of viewing vulnerability as a sign of failure, she saw it as an opportunity for growth and self-compassion. She learned to extend grace to herself during difficult moments, knowing that vulnerability was a testament to her courage and willingness to face the depths of her emotions.

One of the key lessons Emily learned was the importance of self-care as a way to navigate vulnerability. She discovered that taking time for herself, engaging in activities that nourished her mind, body, and soul, and seeking support when needed were essential in maintaining her emotional well-being. Self-care became her anchor, providing her with the strength and resilience to navigate the challenges that vulnerability brought.

In the face of vulnerability, Emily also cultivated resilience. She understood that resilience was not about avoiding pain or adversity but rather about bouncing back and growing stronger from the experiences that tested her. She tapped into her inner strength, drawing upon the lessons she had learned and the support system she had built. When faced with setbacks or moments of uncertainty, she reminded herself of her journey, her progress, and the unyielding spirit that resided within her.

As Emily continued to navigate vulnerability with grace and resilience, she discovered that it was in those moments of vulnerability that she experienced the deepest connections, both with herself and with others. It was through vulnerability that she found the courage to express her authentic self, to share her story, and to inspire others on their own journeys of healing.

Navigating vulnerability became an integral part of Emily's ongoing recovery. It was a continual practice that required patience, self-reflection, and a willingness to step outside of her comfort zone. But with each step, she grew stronger, more resilient, and more connected to herself and those around her.

Emily's journey taught her that vulnerability was not a sign of weakness but a testament to her strength. It was through embracing her vulnerability that she found her truest self and discovered a life filled with authenticity, connection, and joy. And as she continued to navigate vulnerability with grace and resilience, she knew that she was not alone on this journey. She was part of a larger community, united by their shared experiences and their unwavering commitment to healing and growth. Together, they would support one another, celebrate each other's triumphs, and navigate vulnerability with grace, resilience, and a steadfast belief in the transformative power of vulnerability itself.

As Emily continued her journey of healing and recovery, she encountered numerous triggers and temptations that posed a threat to her sobriety. These triggers could be external, such as being in environments associated with her past addiction, or internal, arising from emotional and psychological challenges. Regardless of their origin, Emily knew that confronting and managing these triggers was essential for maintaining her sobriety and staying on the path of healing.

One of the first steps Emily took was to identify her triggers. Through self-reflection and therapy, she gained a deeper understanding of the situations, emotions, and thoughts that had historically led her down the path of addiction. She recognized that triggers could manifest in various forms, such as stress, loneliness, boredom, or specific people and places associated with her past drug use. By identifying these triggers, Emily became better equipped to anticipate and navigate them.

Armed with this awareness, Emily developed coping mechanisms to deal with her triggers. She understood that relying solely on willpower was not enough; she needed practical strategies to help her withstand the pull of temptation. She turned to healthy outlets such as exercise, meditation, and engaging in creative activities. These activities not only served as distractions but also provided her with a sense of fulfillment and emotional release.

Support systems played a crucial role in Emily's ability to face triggers and temptations. She surrounded herself with individuals who understood her journey and were committed to supporting her sobriety. This included close friends, family members, and members of support groups or recovery communities. Through regular communication, open discussions, and sharing her challenges, Emily found solace and strength in the support of those who had experienced similar struggles.

In addition to her support network, Emily leaned on

professional help when needed. She continued therapy sessions, where she could delve deeper into her triggers and develop personalized strategies to overcome them. Therapeutic techniques such as cognitive-behavioral therapy (CBT) and dialectical behavior therapy (DBT) equipped her with tools to challenge negative thought patterns, manage intense emotions, and reframe her relationship with triggers.

As Emily faced her triggers head-on, she discovered the power of mindfulness. By practicing present moment awareness, she cultivated the ability to observe her thoughts and feelings without judgment, allowing them to arise and pass without becoming overwhelmed by them. This mindful approach empowered her to choose healthier responses to triggers rather than reacting impulsively.

Throughout her journey, Emily embraced the concept of self-care as an essential component of managing triggers and temptations. She recognized that taking care of her physical, mental, and emotional well-being was crucial for maintaining her resilience and reducing vulnerability to triggers. Adequate sleep, a balanced diet, engaging in activities she loved, and practicing self-compassion became integral parts of her daily routine.

While facing triggers and temptations required effort and vigilance, Emily understood that it was not a battle she had to fight alone. She learned to reach out for help when she needed it, whether it was talking to a trusted friend, attending a support group meeting, or seeking professional guidance. She realized that asking for support was not a sign of weakness but a testament to her commitment to her sobriety and her ongoing healing.

As time went on, Emily became more adept at recognizing triggers before they gained a stronghold on her. She developed a resilience and strength that allowed her to navigate through challenging moments without succumbing to old patterns. Each successful encounter with a trigger served as a reminder of her progress, reinforcing her belief in her ability to overcome any obstacle.

Emily's journey of facing triggers and temptations was not without its setbacks. There were moments when she stumbled, when the pull of her past seemed too strong to resist. However, she learned to view these setbacks as opportunities for growth and learning. Rather than allowing them to discourage her, she used them as stepping stones to further strengthen her resolve and refine her coping strategies.

In the face of triggers and temptations, Emily remained steadfast in her commitment to her sobriety and her healing journey. She recognized that the path of recovery was not a linear one, but rather a continuous process of self-discovery, growth, and resilience. By facing her triggers head-on, employing coping mechanisms, and relying on her support systems, Emily embraced the power within herself to overcome challenges and live a life of sobriety, fulfillment, and purpose.

As Emily embarked on her journey of addiction recovery and self-discovery, she came to understand that healing was not a destination but a continuous process. It was a realization that she carried with her throughout her life, reminding herself that growth and transformation were ongoing, and that she would encounter both successes and setbacks along the way.

Emily embraced the concept of healing as a journey,

understanding that it was not a linear progression with a defined endpoint. Rather, it was a path of self-discovery, self-awareness, and personal growth that required her commitment and dedication. She accepted that there would be challenges and obstacles to overcome, but she also recognized that each hurdle presented an opportunity for learning and resilience.

Through therapy, self-reflection, and the support of her loved ones, Emily cultivated a deep understanding that healing involved more than just overcoming her addiction. It encompassed all aspects of her life, including her emotional well-being, relationships, and personal fulfillment. She realized that healing required her to confront and address the underlying issues and traumas that had contributed to her addiction, and to create a life that aligned with her values and aspirations.

Emily embraced the idea that healing was not a solitary endeavor. She surrounded herself with a network of support, including friends, family, therapists, and fellow individuals in recovery. These individuals became her pillars of strength, providing encouragement, understanding, and guidance. They reminded her that she was not alone in her journey and that seeking help and leaning on others was not a sign of weakness, but rather an essential part of the healing process.

Throughout her journey, Emily learned to celebrate the successes, no matter how small. Each milestone, whether it was a day of sobriety, a moment of self-awareness, or a positive change in her thought patterns, served as a reminder of her progress and the strength within her. These successes became beacons of hope, fueling her determination to continue on the path of healing and personal growth.

However, Emily also encountered setbacks and moments of difficulty. There were times when old patterns resurfaced, triggering her addiction cravings or challenging her newfound coping mechanisms. In these moments, Emily leaned on her support system, reminding herself that setbacks were a natural part of the healing process. She embraced self-compassion, allowing herself to acknowledge and learn from her mistakes without self-judgment or shame. She understood that setbacks were not a reflection of her worth or her ability to heal, but rather opportunities for growth and recommitment to her journey.

As Emily continued on her path of healing, she developed a deep sense of self-awareness and self-compassion. She learned to listen to her inner voice, to honor her needs and boundaries, and to prioritize her well-being. She recognized that healing required her to let go of old patterns, beliefs, and relationships that no longer served her growth. It involved embracing change, taking risks, and stepping into the unknown with courage and resilience.

Through the ups and downs, Emily remained committed to her personal growth and healing. She understood that healing was not an event that would be completed and checked off, but a lifelong commitment to self-discovery and self-care. She embraced the idea that she was a work in progress, constantly evolving and transforming, and that each day presented an opportunity to learn, grow, and create a life that was authentic and aligned with her values.

As Emily embraced the continuous nature of healing, she

found solace in the process itself. She learned to find joy and fulfillment in the present moment, to appreciate the beauty of her growth, and to remain open to the possibilities that lay ahead. She understood that healing was not about reaching a final destination but about living a life of purpose, resilience, and authenticity.

And so, Emily embraced the journey, knowing that as long as she remained committed to her healing and growth, she would continue to evolve, thrive, and inspire others along the way.

In the midst of her healing journey, Emily learned the profound importance of celebrating the small victories that dotted her path. She realized that each step forward, no matter how seemingly insignificant, was a testament to her resilience, determination, and progress.

Emily understood that healing was not solely marked by major milestones or grand achievements. It was the accumulation of small victories—the moments of courage, self-awareness, and self-care—that truly propelled her forward. Whether it was waking up early and embracing a new morning routine, resisting a trigger or temptation, or practicing self-compassion in the face of a setback, each small victory carried weight and significance.

She learned to pause and acknowledge these moments of triumph, no matter how fleeting they may seem. She celebrated them as meaningful markers of her growth and transformation. By recognizing and cherishing the small victories, Emily cultivated a sense of gratitude and empowerment, fueling her motivation to continue on her healing journey.

Emily also realized that celebrating the small victories

allowed her to shift her focus from the challenges and setbacks she encountered. It provided her with a fresh perspective, reminding her that progress was not solely measured by the distance she still had to go, but also by the distance she had already traveled.

In celebrating the small victories, Emily found solace and encouragement. She no longer dismissed or minimized her achievements, recognizing that they were not to be overlooked or taken for granted. Each small victory represented a triumph over her addiction, a step closer to self-discovery, and a testament to her strength and resilience.

She embraced the practice of self-acknowledgment and self-compassion, giving herself permission to savor and celebrate even the smallest moments of progress. It was through this process that she learned to validate her efforts, honor her growth, and cultivate a sense of self-worth that was rooted in her journey of healing.

Emily also realized that celebrating the small victories extended beyond herself. She shared her triumphs with her support system, allowing them to witness and celebrate alongside her. Their encouragement and recognition became a source of validation and motivation, reinforcing her belief in herself and her ability to overcome challenges.

As Emily continued to celebrate the small victories, she discovered that they served as building blocks for larger successes. The cumulative effect of these moments of triumph fueled her resilience and determination, propelling her forward on her healing journey. They became the fuel that propelled her through the difficult times, reminding her of the progress she had made and the potential that lay ahead.

Through the practice of celebrating the small victories, Emily fostered a positive and empowering mindset. She learned to reframe her perspective and focus on the growth and progress she had achieved, rather than dwelling on her past mistakes or the challenges that lay ahead.

In this way, Emily found solace, inspiration, and strength in celebrating the small victories. She recognized that healing was not a linear process, but rather a series of steps and moments that collectively shaped her journey. By acknowledging and celebrating each small victory, she embraced the power of resilience, self-compassion, and the transformative nature of her healing path.

And so, Emily continued to celebrate the small victories with gratitude and joy, knowing that each step forward brought her closer to a life of wholeness, authenticity, and fulfillment.

9

The Road Less Traveled

As Emily embarked on her healing journey, she discovered the profound solace and introspection that awaited her in the embrace of nature. She yearned to reconnect with the natural world, seeking solace, inspiration, and a sense of peace in its boundless beauty.

Emily understood that nature had a way of captivating her senses and drawing her into the present moment. She would venture into the depths of lush forests, hike along rugged mountain trails, and find herself mesmerized by the rhythmic crashing of ocean waves. In the midst of these awe-inspiring landscapes, she discovered a profound sense of serenity and tranquility.

Nature became her sanctuary, a sacred space where she could leave behind the noise and distractions of daily life and immerse herself in the simplicity and stillness of the natural world. It was in these moments that she found solace and introspection, allowing her to reflect on her journey, process her emotions, and gain clarity and perspective.

Each journey into nature became a pilgrimage of self-discovery. She would find a quiet spot, away from the busyness of the world, and immerse herself in the sights, sounds, and sensations that surrounded her. The gentle rustling of leaves, the vibrant hues of wildflowers, and the caress of a gentle breeze became her companions, whispering messages of healing, resilience, and renewal.

In the embrace of nature, Emily found a profound sense of connection. She realized that she was a part of something much greater than herself—an intricate tapestry of life, where every living being played a vital role. This realization instilled in her a deep sense of humility and gratitude, reminding her of the interconnectedness of all things and the importance of caring for both herself and the natural world.

Nature also became a mirror for Emily's own healing journey. She witnessed the cycles of growth, transformation, and renewal that played out in the natural world, mirroring her own process of healing and self-discovery. She observed how even the harshest winters gave way to vibrant springs, how the most barren landscapes could burst forth with life, and how storms could ultimately give rise to rainbows.

Emily would often find herself sitting beside a babbling brook or under the shade of a towering tree, journal in hand, pouring her thoughts and emotions onto the page. Nature became her co-creator, inspiring her words, lending its wisdom, and providing a safe space for her to express her deepest fears, hopes, and dreams. The natural world became a collaborator in her healing journey, offering its vast beauty and serenity as a canvas upon which she could paint her thoughts and feelings.

In the stillness of nature, Emily learned to listen—to the whispers of her soul, the guidance of her intuition, and the gentle wisdom that emanated from the natural world. She discovered that nature held answers to her deepest questions and served as a wellspring of inspiration, reminding her of her inherent resilience, strength, and capacity for growth.

As Emily journeyed through the road less traveled, she discovered that nature was not merely a backdrop for her healing journey but an active participant in it. The natural world invited her to shed her worries and fears, to release the burdens she carried, and to surrender to the rhythm of life itself. In return, it gifted her with moments of serenity, clarity, and a renewed sense of purpose.

Through her encounters with nature, Emily learned that healing was not solely an internal process but a harmonious dance with the world around her. She embraced the wisdom of the trees, the resilience of the flowers, and the ebb and flow of the tides, recognizing that she, too, possessed the power to heal, to blossom, and to find her own rhythm within the grand symphony of existence.

And so, Emily continued to embark on solitary journeys into nature, finding solace, inspiration, and introspection in its boundless beauty. The road less traveled led her to the hidden depths of her own soul, allowing her to reconnect with her true essence and discover a profound sense of serenity in the embrace of the natural world.

As Emily ventured deeper into the realms of nature, she discovered that the true magic often unfolded in moments of silence and solitude. Amidst the symphony of birdsong and the rustling of leaves, she learned to tune in to the subtle whispers of her own inner voice, finding wisdom and guidance in the depths of her being.

In the stillness of nature, away from the cacophony of everyday life, Emily found refuge from the constant noise and distractions that had once consumed her. She sought out secluded spots, where she could sit in quiet contemplation, enveloped by the gentle embrace of nature's serenity.

At first, the silence felt uncomfortable, as if it were amplifying the echoes of her own thoughts and emotions. But as she embraced the stillness, allowing herself to fully surrender to it, she discovered that silence had a language of its own—a language that transcended words and spoke directly to the core of her being.

In the absence of external noise, Emily's inner world came alive. She became attuned to the rhythm of her breath, the beating of her heart, and the subtle nuances of her own thoughts and emotions. The external world faded into the background, and the internal landscape took center stage.

In those moments of silence, she discovered that she held within her a wellspring of wisdom—a reservoir of insight, intuition, and clarity that had long been overshadowed by the noise of the outside world. The stillness provided the space for her to connect with her deepest truths, to unravel the layers of conditioning and expectations, and to listen to the gentle whispers of her soul.

In the quietude of nature, Emily found solace from the chaos of her addiction and the pressures of society. She realized that the answers she sought were not external but resided within her own being. The silence became a sanctuary for introspection, self-reflection, and self-discovery.

Through the practice of silence, Emily learned to cultivate presence and mindfulness. She discovered that by immersing herself in the present moment, she could fully experience the beauty and intricacy of the natural world around her. The delicate petals of a flower, the dance of sunlight on the water's surface, and the symphony of colors at sunset became vivid and alive, as she allowed herself to be fully present and attuned to the wonders of the present moment.

In the depths of silence, Emily also confronted her fears and insecurities. She discovered that the quietude brought forth the buried emotions and thoughts that had contributed to her addiction. It was in these moments of discomfort and vulnerability that true healing began to take place. With courage and compassion, she faced her inner demons, allowing them to be seen and acknowledged.

Silence became her companion and confidante, a trusted ally on her journey of self-discovery. In the absence of external distractions, she learned to sit with herself in all her complexities—the light and the dark, the joys and the sorrows. She embraced the silence as a space for self-compassion, forgiveness, and self-acceptance.

Through the practice of embracing silence, Emily cultivated a deep sense of inner peace and resilience. She discovered that the noise of the world no longer had the power to define her or sway her from her path of healing. In the quietude, she found the strength to honor her true self, to listen to her intuition, and to follow the whispers of her heart.

As Emily continued to explore the road less traveled, she

carried the gift of silence with her—a sacred space within, where she could retreat whenever she needed solace, clarity, and guidance. In the embrace of silence, she discovered her own inner sanctuary—a place of deep knowing, where the wisdom of her soul could unfold and guide her on the path of self-discovery and healing.

As Emily ventured deeper into the natural world, she found herself captivated by its profound beauty and awe-inspiring majesty. Each step along the road less traveled awakened within her a renewed sense of childlike wonder and curiosity, breathing new life into her weary spirit.

In the presence of towering mountains, expansive valleys, and pristine lakes, Emily felt a stirring deep within her soul. She couldn't help but marvel at the intricate patterns of a butterfly's wings, the delicate petals of a wildflower, and the mesmerizing dance of sunlight filtering through the canopy of trees. The world around her seemed to burst with vibrant colors, sounds, and textures, inviting her to explore, discover, and be fully present in the moment.

With a childlike fascination, Emily began to immerse herself in the small miracles that unfolded before her eyes. She followed the flight of a hummingbird, tracing its path with her gaze, as if trying to capture the essence of its graceful existence. She traced her fingers along the rough bark of ancient trees, feeling a connection to the wisdom held within their ancient roots. She marveled at the symphony of birdsong, listening intently to the melodies that seemed to carry messages from a world beyond her own.

In the embrace of nature's splendor, Emily let go of the jadedness and weariness that had settled in her heart. She embraced the simplicity of being present, of marveling at the wonders that surrounded her. The world became a vast playground, inviting her to explore, to engage her senses, and to reconnect with the innate curiosity that had once defined her.

With each new discovery, Emily's perspective shifted. She realized that there was so much more to life than the struggles and challenges she had faced. The natural world served as a reminder that life was an intricate tapestry of beauty, complexity, and interconnectedness. She marveled at the delicate balance of ecosystems, the interdependence of flora and fauna, and the cycles of life and renewal.

As Emily ventured off the beaten path, she found herself drawn to the hidden corners of the world—the untouched landscapes that held secrets waiting to be uncovered. She traversed rugged trails, crossed babbling brooks, and climbed to lofty peaks, always driven by a sense of curiosity and the desire to witness nature's grandeur firsthand.

In her quest for wonder, Emily also discovered a profound sense of humility. Nature's vastness and timelessness reminded her of her place in the grand tapestry of existence—a small yet significant part of a much greater whole. She realized that her worries, fears, and limitations were merely fleeting in the face of nature's enduring presence. The mountains stood tall, the rivers flowed ceaselessly, and the stars painted the night sky with their eternal glow, offering her a glimpse of something greater than herself.

As she immersed herself in the wonders of the natural world, Emily felt a deep connection to all living beings. She recognized that she was not separate from nature but an integral part of it—a thread woven into the intricate fabric of life. The rhythm of her footsteps echoed the pulse of the earth, and the beat of her heart harmonized with the universal heartbeat that permeated every living creature.

In the presence of nature's grandeur, Emily rediscovered a sense of awe and reverence for life. She reveled in the beauty of a sunrise, the gentle rustling of leaves in the wind, and the delicate dance of raindrops on her skin. She allowed herself to be fully present in these moments, savoring the richness of sensory experiences and finding solace in the simplicity of being alive.

With each encounter with nature's wonders, Emily's spirit was rejuvenated, and her appreciation for the world around her deepened.

As Emily delved deeper into the heart of nature, she couldn't help but notice the remarkable resilience and adaptability displayed by the creatures that inhabited the wild. She witnessed the delicate balance of predator and prey, the instinctual survival strategies of animals, and the harmonious interplay of ecosystems. These observations became a source of inspiration, teaching her valuable lessons about her own capacity for growth and transformation.

In the wilderness, Emily encountered animals that had endured unimaginable hardships—storms, scarcity of food, and constant threats to their survival. Yet, they had found ways to adapt, to thrive even in the face of adversity. Birds built intricate nests to protect their young, camouflaging themselves amidst the foliage to evade predators. Trees withstood fierce winds by bending but not breaking, their roots reaching deep into the earth for stability. The mighty river, flowing with determination, sculpted its path through the rugged terrain, persistently carving through obstacles in its way.

These encounters with nature's resilience served as a mirror to Emily's own journey. She realized that like the animals and the elements, she possessed an inherent capacity to adapt, to overcome obstacles, and to transform. The challenges she had faced, though painful, had also presented opportunities for growth and self-discovery.

Emily observed how animals used their unique strengths and instincts to survive and thrive. The eagle soared high above, surveying the vast landscape with keen eyesight. The spider weaved intricate webs, patiently waiting for its prey. The salmon swam against the current, propelled by an innate determination to reach its spawning grounds. These creatures reminded her of the importance of harnessing her own strengths and innate qualities.

In the wilderness, Emily learned to embrace change as a catalyst for growth. She witnessed the cycle of seasons—the vibrant blossoms of spring, the bountiful harvests of summer, the transformative colors of autumn, and the quiet slumber of winter. Each season had its purpose and beauty, reminding her that change was an inherent part of life's tapestry. Just as the forest shed its leaves in preparation for renewal, she too could release the burdens of her past and make room for new beginnings.

The natural world also taught Emily the importance of interconnectedness. She observed how plants, animals, and ecosystems relied on one another for survival. Bees diligently pollinated flowers, enabling the growth of fruits and seeds. Trees shared resources through an underground network of roots, supporting one another in times of need. This web of interconnectedness highlighted the significance of community, collaboration, and the recognition that we are all interconnected in the tapestry of life.

As Emily embraced the lessons from the wild, she discovered that her journey towards healing and self-discovery mirrored the resilience and adaptability of nature. Just as the wilderness transformed with the changing seasons, she too was capable of shedding old patterns, embracing new possibilities, and growing into her true potential. The challenges she had faced were not insurmountable obstacles but stepping stones on her path to personal growth.

In the wild, Emily found solace and inspiration, understanding that she was not separate from nature but an integral part of it. The lessons she learned from observing the resilience and adaptability of the natural world became guiding principles in her own journey. She realized that by drawing upon her inner strength, harnessing her unique qualities, embracing change, and fostering connections with others, she could navigate life's challenges and thrive.

With each step she took in nature's embrace, Emily felt a deep sense of connection to the wild, to the lessons it offered, and to the endless possibilities that lay ahead. The wisdom of the wilderness permeated her being, reminding her of her own innate resilience and the transformative power of embracing the untamed aspects of life.

As she ventured forth on the road less traveled, Emily carried within her heart the profound lessons learned from the wild. She knew that just as nature flourished in the face of adversity, so too could she find strength, growth, and transformation within herself. With the beauty of nature as her guide, she embraced the journey that awaited her, ready to soar to new heights, guided by the wisdom of the wild.

The Road Less Traveled had brought Emily to breathtaking landscapes and introduced her to remarkable experiences. However, amidst the external exploration, she began to realize that her journey of self-discovery was not solely about the world around her; it was also an inward journey, a profound exploration of her own soul.

As Emily walked along the winding path, she found herself drawn to moments of solitude and introspection. She sought quiet corners, away from the distractions of the external world, where she could delve into the depths of her being. It was in these moments of stillness that she discovered the richness and complexity of her own thoughts, emotions, and desires.

She realized that self-discovery was a multifaceted process that involved peering into the recesses of her soul and unearthing the truths buried within. It required an honest examination of her past experiences, beliefs, and patterns of behavior. She needed to confront the shadows that lurked within, acknowledging the pain, the fears, and the insecurities that had shaped her.

With each step taken on this inner path, Emily encountered different aspects of herself. She met her vulnerabilities head-on, acknowledging the wounds that had been hidden for so long. She embraced her strengths and talents, recognizing the unique gifts that she had to offer the world. And she confronted her own limitations, embracing the humbling truth that growth required the willingness to confront and transcend them.

As she delved deeper into her own soul, Emily discovered that self-discovery was not a linear journey but a labyrinth of emotions, memories, and revelations. It was a process of unraveling the layers that had accumulated over time, peeling back the masks she had worn to fit in or protect herself. She allowed herself to be vulnerable, to experience the full spectrum of her emotions, without judgment or resistance.

In this inner exploration, Emily discovered that self-compassion was an essential companion. She learned to treat herself with kindness and understanding, offering the same love and forgiveness she would extend to a dear friend. It was through this lens of self-compassion that she could truly understand and accept herself, embracing her flaws and imperfections as integral parts of her unique journey.

As Emily continued along the path within, she encountered moments of profound clarity and insight. She gained a deeper understanding of her values, passions, and dreams. She unraveled the stories she had told herself, examining them with a discerning eye and rewriting the narrative to reflect her authentic self. She discovered her deepest desires and aspirations, and with each revelation, she took steps to align her life with her newfound truths.

The path within also led Emily to a place of self-forgiveness. She recognized that holding onto past mistakes and regrets only weighed her down, inhibiting her growth and hindering her from fully embracing the present. Through self-compassion and acceptance, she released the burden of guilt and allowed herself to move forward with a lighter heart.

With each milestone reached on her inner journey, Emily felt a profound sense of liberation and empowerment. The road less traveled had become a path of self-discovery, leading her to a place of authenticity and self-acceptance. She realized that the external world was a reflection of her internal landscape, and by tending to her inner garden, she could cultivate a life of purpose, joy, and fulfillment.

As Emily continued to walk the path within, she understood that self-discovery was not a destination but a lifelong journey. It was a commitment to self-awareness, growth, and continual learning. With each step, she embraced the ever-unfolding layers of her being, knowing that the depths of her soul held infinite possibilities.

On the road less traveled, Emily discovered that the true beauty of self-discovery was not in the final destination but in the transformation that occurred along the way. And as she continued her inward exploration, she marveled at the vastness of her own being, ready to embrace the next chapter of her journey with open arms and an open heart.

10

The Tapestry of Transformation

As Emily embarked on the final chapter of her journey, she found herself in a reflective state, marveling at the intricate tapestry of her life. She could now see how every thread, every experience, and every challenge had woven together to create a masterpiece of transformation. The chapters of addiction and healing had shaped her into a stronger, wiser, and more resilient individual.

Emily traced her finger along the colorful threads that made up the tapestry of her past. She saw the moments of darkness and despair, where addiction had held her captive, entangling her in its destructive web. Yet, as she followed the threads further, she witnessed the emergence of light and hope, where healing had begun to stitch itself into the fabric of her existence.

The tapestry told the story of her journey, the struggles and triumphs, the moments of weakness and the moments of strength. It was a testament to her resilience, the way she had picked up the frayed threads and woven them back together with determination and courage. Each thread represented a lesson learned, a hurdle overcome, and a step forward on the path to her own transformation.

As Emily reflected on the tapestry, she recognized the power of her own narrative. She had the ability to rewrite her story, to shift the focus from the struggles to the triumphs, from the pain to the healing. She saw how her experiences had not defined her but had instead forged her into a person of depth and resilience.

In this moment of reflection, Emily realized that her journey was not just about overcoming addiction but about embracing the transformative power of healing. It was about finding meaning in her experiences, no matter how painful, and using them as stepping stones towards personal growth and self-discovery.

She acknowledged that the tapestry was not just her own, but also a reflection of the countless individuals who had played a part in her healing journey. From the mentors who had offered guidance, to the friends who had provided support, to the strangers who had shown her kindness, their threads intertwined with hers, creating a beautiful mosaic of interconnectedness.

Emily understood that her transformation was not an isolated event but a ripple effect that touched the lives of those around her. Her story had the power to inspire and uplift others who were facing their own battles with addiction and healing. It was a reminder that even in the depths of despair, there was always the possibility of redemption and renewal.

As Emily gazed at the tapestry, she felt a sense of gratitude for the lessons learned and the growth achieved. She saw the beauty in the imperfections, the knots and tangles that added depth and character to the fabric of her life. She realized that her journey had not been linear or without setbacks, but it was precisely those detours and challenges that had shaped her into the person she had become.

With a renewed sense of purpose and gratitude, Emily embraced the final chapter of her journey. She understood that her tapestry was not yet complete, that there were still threads waiting to be woven, stories waiting to be told. She carried with her the lessons learned, the strength gained, and the wisdom acquired, ready to embark on new adventures and weave new chapters into her ever-evolving tapestry of transformation.

And as she took her first step forward, Emily knew that the tapestry of her life would continue to unfold, revealing new patterns, colors, and textures. She was no longer defined by her addiction but by her resilience, her healing, and her unwavering commitment to self-discovery.

As Emily reflected on the intricate tapestry of her life, she realized that her story held the power to inspire and empower others who were grappling with addiction and in need of healing. She understood the immense value of sharing her experiences, vulnerabilities, and triumphs, knowing that her journey could serve as a guiding light for those still lost in the darkness.

With a renewed sense of purpose, Emily embraced her

role as a source of inspiration. She recognized that her story was not meant to be kept hidden but rather to be shared with the world, for there were countless individuals out there who needed to hear that recovery and transformation were possible.

Emily began by reaching out to support groups, community centers, and organizations dedicated to addiction recovery. She offered to share her story, to speak candidly about her struggles, and to provide a beacon of hope for those who felt trapped in the grip of addiction. Through her heartfelt words and unwavering honesty, she aimed to break down the barriers of shame and stigma surrounding addiction, encouraging others to seek help and embark on their own healing journeys.

She spoke of the darkness she had once inhabited, the battles fought within her own mind, and the moments of despair that had threatened to consume her. But she also spoke of the moments of revelation, the turning points that had ignited the spark of change within her. She shared the tools, techniques, and support systems that had aided her recovery, emphasizing that healing was not a solitary endeavor but a collective effort.

Through her storytelling, Emily offered a message of resilience, strength, and possibility. She reminded others that their past did not define them, that there was always the potential for transformation and growth. She instilled hope in the hearts of those who felt hopeless, assuring them that they were not alone in their struggles.

As Emily continued to share her story, she witnessed the impact of her words on individuals who had lost faith in themselves. She received messages of gratitude, stories of personal triumphs inspired by her journey, and testimonials of lives changed for the better. She realized that by embracing her role as an inspiration, she had become part of a larger network of support, connecting with individuals who shared a common goal of healing and self-discovery.

With humility and gratitude, Emily recognized that she was merely a vessel, a messenger of hope for those who needed it most. She understood the responsibility that came with sharing her story and committed herself to being a compassionate listener, an understanding friend, and a guiding force for those who sought her guidance.

Emily's journey of healing and self-discovery became a catalyst for transformation in the lives of others. Through her willingness to be vulnerable and open, she created a ripple effect of empowerment, encouraging individuals to confront their own struggles and take the necessary steps towards recovery.

As she walked this path of inspiration, Emily realized that her journey was not just about her own healing but about empowering others to find their own strength and reclaim their lives. She had become a source of light and hope, a living testament to the power of resilience and the capacity for change.

In sharing her story, Emily discovered that her purpose extended far beyond her own personal growth. She had become a beacon of hope, illuminating the path for others to embark on their own transformative journeys. And as she witnessed the transformation in others, she found a profound sense of fulfillment and fulfillment in knowing that her story had made a difference in the lives of others.

With every word she spoke, every hand she held, and every heart she touched, Emily embraced her role as an inspiration. She knew that her journey was ongoing, that there were still chapters waiting to be written, but she faced the future with unwavering determination, knowing that her story had the power to inspire and empower others to embark on their own paths of healing and self-discovery.

And so, with a heart full of gratitude and a spirit ignited by purpose, Emily continued to share her story, lighting the way for those who needed to find their own strength and reclaim their lives. In doing so, she became a living testament to the transformative power of resilience, compassion, and the unwavering belief in the human spirit's capacity to heal and rise above adversity.

As Emily continued on her journey of healing and self-discovery, she began to witness the profound impact it had on her relationships and community. The transformation she experienced within herself radiated outward, touching the lives of those around her and inspiring them to embark on their own journeys of self-discovery.

Emily's newfound strength, resilience, and authenticity became a beacon of light for her loved ones. Her family and friends witnessed her growth, her unwavering commitment to her well-being, and the joy she now radiated. They saw her shed the shackles of addiction and embrace a life filled with purpose and fulfillment. Inspired by her transformation, they too began to question their own paths, seeking meaning, and searching for their own truths.

Conversations sparked within her inner circle, as loved ones opened up about their own struggles, vulnerabilities, and aspirations. Emily's willingness to share her story created a safe space for others to do the same. She listened with compassion, offering support and guidance when needed. Her experiences became a catalyst for dialogue and connection, deepening the bonds between her and those she held dear.

Beyond her immediate circle, Emily's influence extended to her community. She began participating in local support groups, organizing workshops, and volunteering her time to inspire and empower others who were walking similar paths. The ripple effect of her journey grew wider and stronger, as individuals from all walks of life found solace, encouragement, and hope through her story.

As more people embarked on their own journeys of self-discovery, the collective consciousness of the community began to shift. Conversations around addiction, mental health, and healing became more open, honest, and compassionate. The stigma surrounding these issues began to dissolve as more individuals felt empowered to seek help and support.

Emily's influence extended beyond her immediate surroundings. Her story reached individuals through various channels, including social media, publications, and speaking engagements. She became a voice for those who had yet to find their own, shedding light on the struggles of addiction, the power of healing, and the beauty of self-discovery.

The ripple effect of Emily's transformation continued to spread, inspiring others to embrace their own journeys of self-discovery. The community witnessed the power of vulnerability, resilience, and compassion. They saw how one person's willingness to confront their past and embark on a path of healing could ignite a chain reaction of positive change.

Strangers reached out to Emily, sharing their stories of triumph and transformation, thanking her for being a guiding light in their darkest moments. Some even began sharing their own stories, finding the courage to step out of the shadows and embrace their authenticity. Emily became a symbol of hope and resilience, a testament to the indomitable spirit that resides within each of us.

As she witnessed the impact of her journey on those around her, Emily realized that her healing was not just about herself. It was about creating a ripple effect of transformation, inspiring others to rise above their challenges and live lives filled with purpose and authenticity.

With humility and gratitude, Emily embraced her role as a catalyst for change. She understood that the power of one person's transformation could influence an entire community, fostering a culture of healing and self-discovery. She continued to share her story, knowing that each time she did, she planted a seed of possibility in the hearts of those who listened.

And so, the ripple effect of Emily's journey expanded, touching lives far and wide. Her community became a tapestry of individuals embracing their own paths of healing, growth, and self-discovery. The positive impact she had on others became an everlasting testament to the power of one person's transformation to inspire and uplift an entire community.

In the tapestry of transformation, Emily's journey was a vibrant thread, interwoven with the stories of countless others who found the courage to embark on their own paths of healing. Together, they wove a narrative of resilience, hope, and the enduring power of the human spirit to rise above adversity and create a life filled with meaning and authenticity.

As the chapters of their lives continued to unfold, each person inspired by Emily's story became a thread in the tapestry, adding their unique colors, textures, and experiences to the collective narrative of healing and self-discovery.

And so, the tapestry of transformation continued to grow, ever-evolving, as more individuals stepped into the light of their own authenticity, guided by the radiance of Emily's journey. It was a testament to the infinite possibilities that lie within each of us, waiting to be awakened, embraced, and shared with the world.

In the end, Emily's journey was not just her own. It was a journey of interconnectedness, a testament to the inherent power we possess to uplift and inspire one another. Through her courage, vulnerability, and commitment to her own growth, she ignited a spark of transformation that would continue to burn bright long after her own chapter had reached its conclusion.

And so, the tapestry of transformation unfolded, its vibrant threads weaving together a story of resilience, healing, and the boundless potential of the human spirit.

Emily's journey of healing and self-discovery had been marked by moments of triumph, resilience, and growth. She had overcome numerous obstacles, confronted her past traumas, and embraced her true identity. However, amidst all the progress, Emily came to a profound realization: healing and self-discovery are not linear processes but rather a continuous evolution, filled with imperfections and unexpected turns.

In the earlier stages of her journey, Emily had yearned for a clear path, a step-by-step guide to lead her to complete healing. She had held onto the belief that once she reached a certain point, everything would fall into place and her journey would be smooth sailing. But as time went on, she began to understand that this was an unrealistic expectation.

Life, she realized, was messy and complex. It was not a perfectly scripted story, but rather a tapestry of moments, emotions, and experiences woven together. Just as no tapestry is flawless, neither is the journey of healing and self-discovery. It is in embracing imperfection that true growth and transformation occur.

Emily learned to let go of the notion that she needed to have all the answers or be perfectly healed. Instead, she embraced the beauty of imperfection—the understanding that setbacks and challenges were not signs of failure, but opportunities for growth and learning. She accepted that healing was a lifelong process, with its ups and downs, and that self-discovery was a continuous evolution.

Through embracing imperfection, Emily found freedom. She no longer judged herself harshly for moments of vulnerability or moments when old patterns resurfaced. Instead, she approached these moments with compassion and curiosity, recognizing that they were integral parts of her journey. Each stumble became a chance to learn, to deepen her understanding of herself, and to refine her path.

Emily also began to appreciate the beauty in the imperfections of others. She realized that everyone she encountered was on their own unique journey, with their own struggles and growth. She saw the strength and resilience in their imperfections, recognizing that it was through embracing their flaws that they too found the courage to heal and discover their true selves.

In this newfound perspective, Emily discovered the joy of living in the present moment. She no longer waited for some distant future where everything would be perfect. Instead, she found beauty and fulfillment in the imperfect present—in the messy, imperfect, and wonderfully human moments of life.

She understood that healing and self-discovery were not destinations to reach but rather ongoing processes to be embraced. It was in the journey itself, with all its twists and turns, that she found the richness of experience, the depth of connection, and the growth of her soul.

As Emily continued to embrace imperfection, she became a source of inspiration for others on their own journeys. She shared her story with honesty and vulnerability, encouraging others to let go of the pressure to be perfect and to embrace the imperfect beauty of their own paths. She became a guiding light, reminding others that healing and self-discovery were not about reaching some unattainable ideal, but about embracing their authentic selves and finding peace in the journey.

And so, with each step forward, each stumble, and each moment of growth, Emily embraced imperfection as a reminder that the beauty of life lies in its imperfect, unpredictable nature. She savored the richness of the journey, grateful for the lessons learned, the connections made, and the boundless potential that lay within each imperfect moment.

As Emily stood at the threshold of her new life, she marveled at the profound transformation she had undergone. The shackles of addiction no longer bound her, and she had emerged from the depths of her struggles with a renewed sense of purpose and a burning desire to live life to its fullest.

Gone were the days of hiding behind a mask, pretending to be someone she wasn't. Emily had embraced her true self, flaws and all, and had learned to love and accept every part of her being. The journey of healing and self-discovery had paved the way for her to reclaim her life—a life infused with authenticity, gratitude, and a deep appreciation for the path she had undertaken.

No longer burdened by the weight of her past, Emily felt a lightness in her step and a renewed sense of purpose in her heart. She approached each day with a newfound clarity and determination, no longer taking the simple joys of life for granted. The sun on her face, the laughter of loved ones, the beauty of nature—every experience was a reminder of the preciousness of life and the blessings that surrounded her.

Gone were the days of seeking external validation or numbing her pain with substances. Emily had discovered that true fulfillment came from within—from embracing her passions, nurturing her relationships, and living in alignment with her values. She found solace in the simple pleasures of life—a warm cup of tea, a captivating book, a heartfelt conversation. These small moments became the building blocks of a fulfilling existence.

Emily's journey had not only transformed her own life but

had also rippled out to touch the lives of those around her. Her newfound authenticity and zest for life inspired others to examine their own paths, to question the masks they wore, and to seek their own journeys of healing and self-discovery. She became a beacon of hope—a living testament to the power of resilience, self-love, and the capacity for change.

With addiction behind her, Emily embraced a life of purpose. She channeled her experiences and newfound wisdom into helping others who were still trapped in the clutches of addiction. Through advocacy, support groups, and speaking engagements, she became a voice for change, breaking down stigmas and fostering a community of healing and understanding.

But it wasn't just in the grand gestures that Emily found fulfillment. She discovered that the smallest acts of kindness and compassion had the power to create profound ripples of positivity. A kind word, a listening ear, a helping hand—these were the threads that wove the fabric of her daily life and connected her to the greater tapestry of humanity.

Emily knew that life would still present challenges and obstacles along the way. The road to recovery was not without its bumps and detours. But armed with the lessons she had learned, the resilience she had cultivated, and the support of her newfound community, she faced each hurdle with unwavering determination and an unwavering belief in her own strength.

As Emily stepped into her reclaimed life, she did so with a heart filled with gratitude—for the lessons learned, the growth experienced, and the immense beauty that had blossomed from the ashes of her past. Every day was a gift—a chance to live authentically, to make a positive impact, and to savor the exquisite tapestry of existence.

And so, with a smile on her face and a fire in her soul, Emily embraced the journey ahead, ready to live her life fully, passionately, and with an unwavering commitment to the truth that she had reclaimed.

11

A New Dawn

As the sun rose on the horizon, casting a warm golden glow over the world, Emily stood on the cusp of a new dawn. The journey she had embarked upon, fraught with challenges and triumphs, had led her to this pivotal moment of reflection and anticipation. She marveled at the person she had become, the strength she had found within herself, and the profound transformation that had unfolded.

Looking back on her past struggles, Emily couldn't help but feel a sense of awe at how far she had come. The depths of addiction had tested her resolve, shrouding her in darkness and despair. But she had emerged from that abyss, like a phoenix rising from the ashes, with a newfound resilience and a burning determination to reclaim her life.

The path of healing and self-discovery had not been an easy one. It had demanded her courage, vulnerability, and a willingness to confront the demons that haunted her. There were moments when she stumbled, when the weight of the past threatened to pull her back. But she refused to let those setbacks define her. Instead, she used them as stepping stones, learning from them and using them to fuel her growth.

Through the process of healing, Emily had unearthed layers of herself that had long been buried beneath the scars of addiction. She had peeled back the layers of self-doubt, shame, and fear, uncovering a reservoir of strength, resilience, and compassion. She had embraced her true self, embracing imperfections and celebrating her unique journey.

Now, standing at the precipice of this new dawn, Emily felt a renewed sense of purpose pulsating through her veins. The possibilities that lay before her seemed infinite, and she approached them with an open heart and a boundless curiosity. The world was her canvas, and she was ready to paint it with the vibrant hues of her passions, dreams, and aspirations.

No longer bound by the chains of addiction, Emily was free to explore the vast expanse of life's offerings. She sought experiences that brought her joy and fulfillment—a symphony of laughter, the touch of a loved one's hand, the embrace of nature's beauty. She relished in the simple pleasures that had once been overshadowed by her addiction, savoring each moment with a newfound appreciation.

As she embarked on this new chapter, Emily carried with her the lessons she had learned along the way. She understood that healing was not a destination but a lifelong journey. She knew that setbacks were not failures but opportunities for growth. And she embraced the power of vulnerability, knowing that it was through embracing her own wounds that she could connect with others and make a difference in their lives.

With her heart overflowing with gratitude, Emily vowed to pay it forward. She became a beacon of hope for others who were still mired in the depths of addiction, offering support, guidance, and understanding. She shared her story, not as a tale of despair, but as a testament to the resilience of the human spirit and the power of transformation.

And as the new dawn bathed the world in its gentle light, Emily took a deep breath, ready to step into the unknown with courage and conviction. She knew that challenges would inevitably arise, but she was armed with the strength she had cultivated and the unwavering belief in her ability to navigate the twists and turns of life.

With each new day, Emily would rise with a sense of purpose, guided by the wisdom she had gained on her journey. The past would no longer define her; it would serve as a reminder of her resilience and the profound growth she had experienced. The future held limitless possibilities, and she was ready to seize them with open arms.

As the final pages of her story turned, Emily embraced the new dawn that awaited her—a tapestry of moments waiting to be woven, adventures yearning to be embarked upon, and a life ready to be lived to its fullest. With gratitude in her heart and a spark of joy in her eyes, she stepped forward, ready to embrace this new chapter, where the possibilities were as vast as the sky and the beauty of life unfolded with every step she took.

David Olubiyi, a fresh and promising author hailing from Alberta, Canada, presents his compelling literary fiction masterpiece, 'The Fragments Within.' With an innate passion for delving into the human experience, Olubiyi weaves a tapestry of addiction, healing, and self-discovery that resonates deeply with readers. Drawing inspiration from his own journey and a family of four, Olubiyi's empathetic storytelling captures the complexities of the human spirit's resilience and the transformative power of embracing one's true self. His previous works, including 'Building Resilience: Nurturing your child's inner strength,' 'Rebuilding Love,' and 'Awakening your True Self,' showcase his commitment to exploring themes that resonate universally. 'The Fragments Within' is a testament to Olubiyi's dedication to crafting narratives that inspire growth, empathy, and a renewed sense of purpose.

www.ingramcontent.com/pod-product-compliance
Lightning Source LLC
Chambersburg PA
CBHW040536170726
48295CB00012B/486